Sam Ayertey was born in
He was educated at Mount
of Ghana. On completion, h   ... a grant for post-
graduate studies in literature at Atlanta University, Georgia.
He obtained the M.A. degree in 1975. Sam lectured at
Spelman College, Atlanta, before returning to his native
country. There, he taught for a few years and relocated to
Britain to pursue a course in order to satisfy his quest for
writing. He actually started writing at the University of
Ghana. There he won two academic prizes for short story
and verse writing. *Transformation of a Village* is his first
major work. Sam Ayertey spends his leisure times listening
to music and watching movies, literary and sporting
activities. He is married and blessed with three children.

Sam Ayertey

TRANSFORMATION OF A VILLAGE

AUSTIN MACAULEY PUBLISHERS™

LONDON • CAMBRIDGE • NEW YORK • SHARJAH

Ordering Information
Quantity sales: Special discounts are available on quantity purchases by corporations, associations, and others. For details, contact the publisher at the address below.

Publisher's Cataloging-in-Publication data
Ayertey, Sam
Transformation of a Village

ISBN 9781685624743 (Paperback)
ISBN 9781685624750 (ePub e-book)

Library of Congress Control Number: 2023920561

www.austinmacauley.com/us

First Published 2024
Austin Macauley Publishers LLC
40 Wall Street, 33rd Floor, Suite 3302
New York, NY 10005
USA

mail-usa@austinmacauley.com
+1 (646) 5125767

Chapter 1

John Wayo was the second son of Teye and Dede. His father was a wealthy local farmer, one of the people of Adoma who first embraced western education. As a result of that, all his six children but two were educated. In order to make this possible, he allowed some of them to live with relatives at Kesua to enable them have access to western education.

After Wayo's secondary education, he went to a college in the city where he studied Public Relations. He was a brilliant man and so it was no surprise that he ended up getting a job as a Personnel Officer with United Africa Company, popularly known as U. A. C., one of the biggest textile companies in the country.

He was the embodiment of a real gentleman. He never smoked or drank alcohol. And apart from the interest he had in sports and community work during his leisure time, his only concern was his job and the welfare of his wife and their two children. Because of his simple lifestyle, he did not want to live in the heart of the city where his company, U. A. C., was situated. Instead, he chose to live in one of the quietest and more environmentally friendly suburbs of the city, and he was happy to drive or take the bus to work and back every day.

In that environment, he hoped to train and educate his children beyond the education his father gave him. As far as he, himself, was concerned, his aim was to work as assiduously and honestly as possible to earn him a promotion to the highest level.

He was therefore pleased to hear from management that plans were in progress to send him abroad for further studies so that when the Personnel Manager was ready to leave the country for good, he could take over his position.

In spite of his great concern for his work and family, Wayo did not forget his birth place, Adoma, and his dear family. He always made sure he visited his parents every month and stayed with them over the weekend, taking with him any affordable present he could get. While there, he helped his parents in anything they were doing and always took part in any community work taking place at the time. Because of this, many people in Adoma knew and liked him.

When Nene Tsatsu 11, the traditional chief of Adoma died, the elders and kingmakers decided not to install illiterate people as chiefs anymore. They were of the belief and conviction that an educated chief could help bring more developments to the village because of the variety of ideas he acquired in school. But in order to have an educated chief, they had to change the rules governing the selection and installation of chiefs.

The ascendancy to the Stool, the official seat of the chief, was not through inheritance since the position was not a monarchy. Rather, it was through a selection of a candidate from any of the two royal families, in a rotational pattern, and an approval by a council of elders and kingmakers. But in the search for a successor to the late chief, the rotational method was, with the agreement of both families, abolished unanimously. That was to pave the way for any person from any of the royal families who was more qualified at the time, to be selected and approved for installation as a chief. As a result of this procedural change, John Wayo was popularly nominated and when a vote was cast, his selection was approved with a big majority.

But when Wayo's choice, as the new chief-elect, was communicated to his parents, they objected to it vehemently. They did not want their son to be a chief and suffer the same fate that ended their brother's life prematurely. They were of the belief that the late Nene Tsatsu 11's death was caused by his enemies through black magic. During those days, the use of black magic, especially for destructive purposes, was very rife. In addition to that, they did not want their son to leave the work he was doing in the city and move down to the village to be a chief. The elders and the kingmakers appreciated the parents' concern but they appealed to them to reconsider their decision in the interest of the village.

That same week, a delegation of elders was sent to the city to inform Wayo officially of his popular choice as the next chief of Adoma. He was alerted that the elders were coming and so he stayed at home on the day of their arrival and gave them a warm welcome. He treated them with great respect and hospitality. There were plenty of drinks and food, as custom demanded, and the discussion was lively and hearty. But the mood changed suddenly when the elders told him why they had come to visit him.

Wayo thanked them for the visit and his choice to be the next chief of Adoma. But he added politely that he was not looking for another job and that he was happy and satisfied with the work he was doing. Besides, he had many dreams about himself and his family and being a chief at the village was not one of them. So he advised them to go back and choose another person. The elders tried in many ways to convince him to agree to be the next chief. But Wayo insisted that he did not want to be a chief and nothing would make him change his mind. So the elders had to leave, very disappointed.

Back at the village, the elders and the kingmakers received the outcome of the visit to Wayo with great regret and disappointment. Some of them were even annoyed that Wayo should refuse the call to be their chief. A meeting was held again and it was decided that another delegation should be sent to Wayo, hoping that he would change his mind. The leader tried to explain to him that his nomination was based on special reasons and that it was a popular one. But Wayo was not in the mood to listen to anything they said to convince him. In order to get rid of them, he told them he had an important business to attend to for an hour and so he asked permission to leave. He promised coming back soon but he never returned as promised. By the time he came back, the elders had left, back to the village.

They and, indeed, a great number of people were not happy with the two abortive missions. A meeting was convened immediately and a decision was taken to send another delegation to Wayo. This time, members were charged with more powers and given the authority to arrest Wayo, in accordance to tradition, and perform the preliminary ritual on him, if he proved difficult again. So the royal priests went to the royal grove, cut a few leaves from the okli herbs and pounded them into pulp. This was mixed with the blood of a sheep and poured into a little bottle. Then it was given to the members of the delegation to be used on Wayo.

According to the custom of Adoma people, once the blood of a sheep or the content of the bottle was sprayed on the feet of prospective chief, he could not refuse to be installed chief any more. If he dared refuse it, the gods would be angry with him and he would not be prosperous in life. It was said that some time ago, a man ran away after the initial ritual had been performed on him, and he became mad afterward.

A new member, Nanor, was added to the delegation and made leader of the team. He was an influential and powerful speaker, one of the few fortunate people who first went to school. He reached only standard six though, but he was always boastful of his great knowledge. When he was a primary school teacher in the village, he made some trips to the city and so people considered his inclusion in the team as a wise one. Other members included Huno and Okete, both of them kingmakers, and Kwao, a family representative.

As usual, Wayo got to know that this empowered delegation was coming because there were informants in the village who were giving him information. So he decided to avoid them. The night before the arrival of the people, he had a discussion with his wife in which he told her he would not come back home after work until the people had come and gone. He confided in his wife that he would be a guest of his friend, Saki, but she should tell the people that he was out of town, on a trek.

So early in the morning, Wayo left home. He did not even take his favorite breakfast of white porridge and a slice or two of bread stuffed with fried eggs. Instead of taking the more direct tarmac road to the bus stop, he took a meandering path through the town. He got to the bus stop just as a bus was about to depart. He quickly jumped onto it. While the bus glided down the hill, Wayo thought over his plans again and appraised them. He would stay away from his house for some time. He hoped that members of the third delegation, like the first two, would return to the village if they came and did not meet him.

The bus negotiated a curve and sped on. In a few minutes' time, he had to disembark at the next bus stop. His friend's house was behind that bus stop. He hoped that Saki would be at home to welcome him. Soon the bus reached the bus stop but because nobody had indicated that he would get out, and no one was there to get on board, the driver continued to press the accelerator.

Only Wayo had to alight at this bus stop but he was so engrossed in thoughts that he forgot to press the bell to alert the bus driver. All along the road was very smooth and the passengers had had a delightful ride. But a few meters away from the bus stop, the bus went into pot-holes. So the driver had to apply the brake on reaching each pot-hole which made the passengers, especially those standing, crash into each other vigorously.

It was at this time that Wayo came back to his senses. He got up suddenly and looked forward and backward. Then he pressed the bell and shouted: 'Bus stop, I will alight here, driver.' Some of the passengers turned and looked at him.

'Stop for me, driver, I'm getting down here,' he continued. This made some of the people in the bus give a cynical laugh.

The driver replied that he had already passed the stop and advised him to wait until the next stop.

Wayo then left his seat and elbowed his way through the standing passengers to the exit door. Luckily for him, there was a traffic-jam and the driver had to slow down. He took advantage of this hold-up, forced the door open and desperately jumped down, cursing as he walked back. Some of the passengers turned and looked at him, holding him in derision.

He had to trek about three hundred meters back to the last bus stop and then to his friend's house. By the time he got there, he was very exhausted. This, coupled with annoyance, made him worn-out. He drifted to his friend's door and knocked. Saki was surprised to see him at that time.

'What brings you here this morning? Are you not going to the office?' asked Saki.

'Let me enter first before you start asking me questions,' responded Wayo. He walked past him into the sitting room and found himself a seat. Saki closed the door and followed him. He stared at his friend for a while and then asked: 'Is anything wrong with you? You look very worried.'

'It was that idiot, that bus driver who refused to stop for me and so I had to walk all the way back,' responded Wayo.

'Maybe you did not alert him early enough.'

'I did, Theo. He just did not pay attention to the bell. And because he did not listen, I had to walk all the way back from the T junction.'

'Well, you have to forget about it,' Saki advised and moved to the dining table.

'I hope you will not mind joining me at table?' he asked his friend. That was a welcome invitation. Wayo answered in the affirmative and moved to the table.

Saki then called his wife and asked her to come and serve him. It was brown porridge, popularly known as Tom Brown, prepared from milled roasted corn, and served with slices of bread. It was Saki's favorite for breakfast. When they finished their meal, Wayo cleared his throat and told his friend about the royal delegation from his village.

'I was informed yesterday in confidence that another royal delegation is coming to me today.'

'Is it about the chief matter?'

'Yes…They are, in fact, worrying me.'

'Then why can't you be bold and tell them you are not interested in being a god-damned chief? What do you gain from being a chief, anyway?'

'Nothing, Theo. It is just a waste of one's dreams. I told the previous delegations that I didn't want to be a chief and that they should look for somebody else. Why another group of people are coming to me again is what I don't understand.'

'Look, John, this is not a matter of dodging them or going on self-exile. You have to meet those who are coming and make your position clear to them again. Tell them uncompromisingly that you are not interested in being a chief, a village chief for that matter. You are already in a gainful employment, aren't you?'

'You are right. But I have to stay clear of the people who are coming. I hear they have been charged with the responsibility of arresting me and taking me home to be crowned.

'Arrest you? What offence have you committed?'

'No offence. This is the custom of my people. When one is chosen to be a chief and he refuses, he is taken by force. I hear those who are coming today are asked not to fail to bring me home. So I have to avoid them.'

It was time for both of them to leave for their respective working places and so they had to discontinue the discussion. Wayo would come back to be a guest of Saki for a night or two.

They left the house and hailed a taxi. After a few minutes' ride, Saki alighted. His work place was not very far from where he lived.

Wayo still had a kilometer and a half to go. He had to bend his body forward in the car because of his height. This made him look like a hunch-back. His round face and broad shoulders resembled those of a boxer. Another thing very remarkable about him was his well-trimmed moustache. After his secondary school education, he did a course in Public Relations and worked at Goku Industries for some years as a Personnel Officer before joining the staff of United Africa Company.

Wayo was a man of principles. He had vowed to take his father's ways of life and never deviated from them. Like his father, he neither smoked nor drank alcohol. His life was so regimented that people who did not know him well always mistakenly took him to be a boring man.

He was very time-conscious and so, very often, one would hear him querying people about their attitudes to time. To him, there was nothing like "African punctuality" as people used to say. 'Time is time everywhere in the world,' he used to tell people. Therefore he wanted everyone to stick to time and observe it accordingly. One day, he had to leave his wife at home because she was delaying him and he did not want to be late to a function to which both of them were invited.

At home, everything was so arranged in order that even a blind man could be sent for anything that was needed. Whenever a thing was used it had to be put back at the place it was taken. He wanted things to be at their right places all the time, and so any time he found something at an odd place, he complained. Because of this, he was associated with the expression: 'Things must be where they belong.' To him, things must be picked when needed and not looked for, and that only lost things had to be looked for.

The taxi pulled up in front of United Africa Company with a jerk which infuriated him. However, he did not complain. There were so many problems weighing on him that he did not want to indulge in a confrontation with a taxi driver. He disembarked and walked straight into the building and up to his office. Just before closing time, he received a secret message from his wife that the people from his village had arrived. Therefore, after work he went straight to his friend's house as already planned. He would be there for as long as the people stayed in town. Saki was already in the house when he got there. So they sat down together to discuss the new developments:

'Now that the members of the delegation are in, what are the next steps to be taken?' Saki asked.

'I will continue to be here, if you don't mind. I know after a day or two, they will be fed up and go back to the village. If they stay longer, they may run out of funds and that might force them to leave. I asked Naki to tell them I had gone on a trek'

'As I have said before, this will not solve the problem and give you a peace of mind. I still think you should confront them and make things clear to them.'

'They will not listen. They say I am the rightful person and that my education will make me a better chief.'

'Let me tell you, they just want to waste your life plans, and I don't want that to happen to you. There is so much envy and hatred surrounding the office of a chief. Sometimes, black magic is used to get rid of chiefs. I know many chiefs who did not last long on the stool.'

'I am aware of that.'

'Then you have to be careful. In the first place, the progressive chiefs are, in most cases, weighed down and made impotent by unwarranted restrictions in the name of tradition. Again, chiefs are always surrounded by hypocrites whose stock-in-trade is back-biting and litigation. This kind of attitude completely cripples the enlightened chief and shatters his lofty ideas and aspirations. If he is lucky, he is removed from the stool under flimsy charges. If he is not, his life is cut short. The lives of chiefs are marked by vicissitudes, John. I want my

15

life to be in my own hands. This is the reason why I want you to go to them.'

'You do not understand. My going there will mean I am surrendering myself to them.'

They were quiet for a few minutes and then Saki broke the silence. 'Well, I pray that your plan works well for you. You have good prospects at the U.A.C. and I do not want you to lose your job there. Your people cannot make you a chief against your human rights to refuse it.'

With this, they retired to bed. But Wayo could not sleep. His mind was too saturated with various thoughts to enable him sleep. First, he thought of the circumstances leading to running away from his own home. He could not imagine himself relinquishing his job and becoming a chief. Then he thought of his wife and children. His thoughts faded into prayers in which he appealed to God to find him a way to avoid being made a chief. Then finally he fell asleep.

When the members got to Wayo's house, they were received courteously by Naki, his wife, who informed them that her husband had gone on a trek. Nanor was the first to express his doubt:

'Gone on a trek?' he asked.

'Yes, my elder.'

'Where is he gone to?'

'He is gone to Tama.'

'Gone to Tama?' Kwao asked in disbelief. He has never been there before,' he continued.

'He was there before, Sir. Last year, too, he went there at this same time.'

'When is he coming back,' asked Huno.

'He will be away for a fortnight.'

None of the members asked any more questions. But considering what happened during the previous missions, they did not take what Naki was telling them to be true. They knew it was a plan to throw them off. So they decided to wait for Wayo. Even if he would be away for a month, they were ready and well-equipped to wait for him.

Their major problem was accommodation. Wayo was occupying an apartment containing only two bedrooms and a parlor. This obviously could not contain all of them. Naki suggested a motel nearby, since they wanted to wait but Nanor objected to it.

He rather asked Naki if she could spread mats on the parlor for them to lie on which she was not in favor of.

She found the request unacceptable to her and she made this known to all of them. She had a genuine reason for her objection: they were her fathers and so she would not let them sleep on the floor. But Nanor insisted that they would not sleep anywhere else. He, too, had his own reasons.

So Naki had to throw in the towel and accept their request. She was from a reputable family and as a wife of Wayo she did not want to argue with her husband's visitors. That would mean disrespect for them. So she accepted the money she was given for their meals and started putting things together to make them as comfortable as possible.

Every day, after breakfast, Nanor and his friends would go and sit under a gigantic neem-tree in front of the house. The leaves of this tall tree formed a canopy of the heavens, making the place very cool. Apart from its coolness, the area was also strategic to them. They could clearly see who came in or out of Wayo's house. Sometimes they would be watching passers-by and traffic, and then doze off.

By the third day, they became bored and tired of their long stay in the city. All of them complained of pains in their bodies and expressed their boredom in various ways. Okete considered their long stay in the town a forced confinement and attributed the pains in their bodies to sleeping on the floor. He complained bitterly about the food too. He was fed up with tea and bread in the morning and rice or kenkey in the evening. These according to him were for coastal people. He wanted his favorable boiled plantain served with kotomire-green leaves' stew; or cassava or cocoyam fufu with palmnut soup in the evening.

Huno was more disgusted with the boredom. He was not used to just eating and sitting down or sleeping all the time. 'That was a routine for lazy or sick people,' he said. So he complained that his continuing stay in the town was making him sick while his farms remained unattended to.

Kwao was very impatient and uneasy but he did not talk much. He hoped that Wayo would return home early from wherever he was so that they could go back home with him. As a family representative, he had to protect the family's image and respect.

Nanor was not bothered at all. Occasionally, he would leave his colleagues and stroll up and down to survey the area. One day he went too far and missed his way and so he could not trace his steps back. If he had not met a Good Samaritan who directed him back home, he would have been lost. When his concerned friends asked him why he kept very long in town, he lied to them that he was just enjoying himself.

One day, he decided to go to the city center and asked Okete to accompany him. Many years ago, he worked there for a contracting company and so he could still remember some places. As they went from one place to another, he talked to friendly people and sought information about people he had known before. But to his displeasure, nobody had any idea about any of the people he wanted to meet.

The next day, Nanor and Okete left for the city center again. This time they went to Osu where he had stayed before. After spending about an hour admiring the tall buildings, they fell into the company of a man who said he was from Adoma. Nanor got to know from this man that an old friend of his was still in the city. He was very delighted to meet this friend when they were directed to him. They talked enthusiastically about their experiences in the village and then in the city where they worked together. Later on, a friend of the host joined them and Nanor entered into a conversation with him:

'How is the city now?'

'It is very hectic, full of struggles. But I like working here.'

'We still enjoy our simple life, full of love and warmth. By the way, where do you work?'

'United Africa Company. I am a clerk there,' the man responded.

'Is that what people call U.A.C.?'

'Oh yes. That is the short form. You just say U.A.C. and everybody will know what you are talking about. We are textile specialists. We supply the best Dumas cloths to the whole country.'

'A cousin of mine works there.'

'Oh, then I must know him. What is his name?'

'Wayo, John Wayo.'

'Ye----s, I know him. Everybody knows him. He is the Personnel Officer. Very soon, the Personnel Manager, the white man, will leave the country on retirement and John will replace him.'

'I hear he is on trek to Tama.'

'Gone on trek? He was at work yesterday. I am sure I saw him, even today.'

'I see. I am not surprised.'

'Is there any problem?'

'There is no problem, my brother. Then he must be back home by now. Thank you for the information.'

Nanor and Okete were extremely delighted about the information they got. Their suspicion that Naki was not telling them the truth was confirmed. When they got home, they told the other members of the delegation about their discovery. But she was not confronted. The following day, the group left the house, telling Naki that they were going on sightseeing. They hailed a taxi which took them straight to the premises of the U.A.C. It was a tall building, the tallest in the area. There they introduced themselves to the gateman as a delegation from Adoma and requested to see the Manager. Asked why they wanted to see him, Nanor replied that it was a business matter which only the Manager could handle for them.

Unsuspectingly, the gateman called another man and asked him to take the visitors to the manager. They were taken up a flight of stairs to the fifth floor. As they climbed up, Nanor felt his legs wobbling and wondered whether workers always did that climbing. By the time they reached the fifth floor all of them became exhausted. Nanor did not hide his feelings.

'Do you have elderly workers here?' he asked the attendant.

'We have a few of them,' he replied.

'And do they do this climbing exercise every day?'

'Oh! You mean the climbing of the stairs? We have an escalator which is presently out of order.' The man explained.

'I see. You better see that it is repaired before I come here again.' Nanor added jokingly.

The manager was very busy when the visitors were led into his office. He was not given prior information as it was the normal procedure. And so he wondered why they had come to see him.

Nanor apologized to the manager for their intrusion and introduced his colleagues to him in his staccato English. Then he began to tell him why they were there. Things had to be done without undue delay; otherwise Wayo would get to know of their presence in the building and escape.' We have come to ask permission from you and take John Wayo home to our elders,' Nanor continued.

'You are here to take Mr. Wayo away?'

'Yes, the people of Adoma need him urgently. He is to be installed chief of Adoma.'

'They want to make him a chief?' The manager was confused. There was a brief silence during which he surveyed all the four members from head to toe. Then he continued, 'I do not understand. By the way, is Mr. Wayo aware of your coming?'

'Yes, he is,' responded Nanor.

'But to be frank with you, I do not want to miss him. He is very important to the Company. Very soon, he will take over the management of the whole personnel department.'

'Manager, his people need him. It is a traditional matter. He is to succeed the late Chief,' Nanor added.

There was a pause again. The Manager sat back in his chair. He bent his head forward and chocked his forehead with his right hand placed on the arm of the chair. After a few minutes, he changed his posture and broke the silence:

'I do not want to interfere with your noble tradition but I think this is not going to augur well for Mr. Wayo.'

'I know how you feel but he has to go and serve his people. It is a service he cannot refuse.'

The manager knew there was nothing he could do. So he rang a bell, and a young man entered.

'Call me Mr. Wayo.'

'Yes, Sir.'

A few minutes later the door opened. Wayo stopped short as soon as he recognized the visitors. He could not make up his mind whether to proceed or return. The manager realized the situation and so he rescued him from his dilemma. Wayo. I am sure you know these people.' There was an exchange of apprehensive glances between him and the visitors, and then he said, 'yes.'

'Well, they are here to take you home to your people. They…'

'I am not going anywhere. I have told them already that I do not want to be a chief.' Wayo's voice rose in a crescendo as he spoke and by the time he finished, he was breathing heavily.

'Be calm Mr. Wayo and let them know your position again. Maybe, this time, they may understand you,' interrupted the Manager.

Under the prevailing circumstances, Nanor decided to act immediately. He did not want to take chances. So he got up and took the little bottle from his pocket. Then as if he wanted to present something, he galloped forward with the speed of a hare and sprayed the traditional concoction on Wayo's feet, saying: 'This is what connects you with our ancestors and the people of Adoma, and makes you their chief.'

The whole action was so fast that it took him off-guard. He sprang up in anger and raised his right hand up as if to punch Nanor. But the presence of the Manager apparently unnerved him. He stared at him and all the members of the royal delegation and screamed: 'You have ruined me, you have ruined my life, oh God.'

'Your life is not ruined, Wayo. You know this ritual is in conformity with our tradition, which I am sorry, we are forced to perform here,' Nanor responded.

In the process of sprinkling the concoction on Wayo's feet, some of it dropped on the flashy rug which covered the floor from wall to wall. This was actually in accordance with tradition.

Some of the concoction must drop on the floor to connect the incoming chief to the ancestors and land he is going to rule.

The manager noticed the mess when Wayo eventually sat down and exclaimed with displeasure: 'My floor, my floor, you have messed up my floor.' He rose to examine the stain.

'I am very sorry,' Nanor apologized. 'I had to perform this very important rite in the circumstances in which I find myself.'

'Here in my office?' the manager fumed. The other members of the group had seen a white man before but not at that close range and not in that fury. There was a frozen silence for a few seconds and then Nanor stood up to speak.

'Once again, I am sorry. You see, I had to perform this rite here to prevent Wayo from running away from the stool of Adoma…for the third time. With this ritual, he cannot refuse the stool anymore. If he dares, he will never be a normal person again. The ancestors will not take it lightly.'

While the encounter between the Manager and Nanor was going on, Wayo sat in his chair, his head bent down speechless. When Nanor asked the Manager if there was anything he would say before their departure, he declared:

'I am sorry he is forced to leave the Company under circumstances beyond my control. He has worked with us devotedly and something surely has to be done for him. But this is not the time for any arrangement.' Then, turning to Wayo, he said: 'Mr. Wayo, you may come back any time you are free for your entitlements to be worked out for you. I hope you are going to be a selfless and impartial chief.'

Nanor was very elated on hearing what the manager said about Wayo. He thanked him for his cooperation and his assessment of him. This was followed by a handshake involving the other members. Just as Nanor was thinking of how to ask Wayo to get up and leave with them, the manager saved the situation. He moved forward and hugged him, and gave him an encouraging advice. Then he prayed for him, asking God to grant him good health and wisdom to rule his people.

Chapter 2

The news of Wayo's home coming spread like bushfire to every nook and cranny of Adoma, amidst mixed feelings. Nobody could say who exactly brought it but everywhere, groups of people could be seen discussing Wayo's imminent arrival.

'So they have got him at last.'

'Yes. I hear he played some tricks again but he was eventually cornered at his manager's office.'

'What? Is the manager not a white man?'

'I am not very sure but I hear he was invited to the manager's office and Nanor performed the preliminary traditional rites on him, and that made him unable to run away.'

'I know it! I know that with the inclusion of Nanor in the delegation, Wayo would not be able to run away from the people of Adoma anymore. So when are they bringing him home?'

'I hear they will be in any time from now. I just passed by the palace, the chief's residence, and I could see many people going in and out.'

Since time immemorial, there had been two royal families in the village of Adoma from which chiefs were selected alternatively. Some years back, a serious crisis erupted which almost tore the village apart. When the previous chief died, each family presented a candidate and both insisted that their candidate should be accepted by the kingmakers. None of them was prepared to compromise in spite of appeals from many concerned people. The village then became divided into two, each supporting a candidate. This escalated the situation. So the candidate who was more popular with a majority of the people could not be installed. An attempt was made but the installation had to be stopped because of the strife that erupted.

The local authority police could not contain the chaotic situation and reinforcement had to be brought from the district headquarters at Kesua. Even with the reinforcement, it took the police three days before they could bring normalcy to the village. But the year passed with Adoma not having a chief.

The following year, an agreement was reached between the two royal families and the kingmakers. Under this accord, both families reaffirmed their commitment to rotate the choice of a candidate for the office of the chief between the two families again, and to respect each other's choice. This had been followed to the letter up to the installation of the last chief.

When the chief died, another accord was reached, making education and experience the main requirements for a candidate to be accepted as a chief, regardless of which royal family he was from. This meant that the rotational method was abolished. Any educated and more experienced person from any of the two families could therefore be chosen as a chief. The people were of the belief that an educated chief would give them better leadership, and could lead them to develop Adoma faster. This was the reason why Wayo was chosen to be the chief when his uncle died.

A few people from the other royal family were naturally not fully in agreement. Akortorku, for an example, took part in all the deliberations but when it came to the final vote, he abstained. But many people were not surprised. He was a landowner and very rich but he was very controversial. He always wanted things to be done his own way and when things did not go the direction he wanted, he would resort to other means. As a result of that character of his, many people did not like him.

Some members from Wayo's family, especially his mother, were also not in support of his choice as the next chief of Adoma. But they had a different reason for their objection. They did not want their son to be made a chief since he was already in a gainful employment and very happy where he was. In spite of this opposition, the kingmakers went ahead with proceedings, hoping that in due course, those concerned would change their mind and support his installation.

Members of the delegation brought Wayo to Adoma in the evening. He was taken straight to the palace, the chief's residence, under the care of the kingmakers. His relative, Kwao, was left behind to help Naki in putting his valuables in order before proceeding to Adoma. On his way to his house that evening, Nanor bumped into Akortorku. Even though he told him he was tired and exhausted, he engaged him in a conversation:

'So you are back.'

'Yes. We brought Wayo home not quite long ago.'

'You have now achieved your aim.'

'It is not my aim. It is our aim. All of us took part in the decision to have an educated chief in the interest of Adoma.'

'All of us indeed. Are you not one of the people who brought the idea and stood firmly in support of it?'

'That's true. But the rest of the people, including you, approved it. Now almost every chief everywhere can read and write. You see, education is very important in this modern world.'

'You know what you are going to gain personally. But I call it a conspiracy. You have deprived us of the chance to have a chief from our family. You will regret it.'

'Akortorku, you cannot say that now. You are being selfish. You have to think of Adoma as a whole, and the one who can give us the development we need.'

'You can say what you like. You people think because you have book people in your family you are the wisest. But you cannot lord it over us.'

'You are mistaken, Akortorku. Let us not think of divisive matters now. This is the time when we have to find out how to make Wayo a good chief. As I have already told you, I am very tired and so let me go home.'

Nanor was very unhappy with the impression Akortorku had created about him. He was one of the two representatives from the Otu royal family who took part in all the meetings that approved the nomination of Wayo. Therefore to turn round and criticize his selection, even before his installation, to him, amounted to a betrayal of trust. However, Nanor was optimistic that his apparent change of mind would be short-lived and so it would not adversely affect Wayo's coronation.

When Wayo's mother was told that his son had been brought and that he was in the palace, she became upset. She wanted him to be brought to his own home first but the kingmakers thought that would be a risk. So, together with a few of her supporters, she went to the palace and asked the kingmakers to release her son to her. But her request was turned down. She was told Wayo was no more her son alone but also a son of the village of Adoma, and that was the "last straw that broke the camel's back".

Dede got infuriated. And together with her male relatives they tried to force their way into the palace. This attracted many people's attention, something the elders did not want to happen. So frantically, they appealed to Wayo's mother to allow the kingmakers to carry on with their duties. Eventually, after some time of diplomatic negotiations, his mother agreed to cooperate with the kingmakers. So another possible strife was averted.

When normalcy was restored, they entered into a dialogue with her mother again. And after a long time of behind-the-scene talks, Dede agreed to relinquish her opposition to her son's installation and then she gave him her blessings.

Having secured his mother's consent and cooperation in the installation of Wayo as chief of Adoma, the kingmakers became happily free to go ahead with all the required rites. He was immediately confined. Nobody was allowed to visit him except his mother and wife. His attendants were the kingmakers. They were seven in number, and they attended to and instructed him in various aspects of chieftaincy matters. He was taught the rules about the stool, the official seat he was going to sit on; how to put on the traditional cloths, the native sandals and how to hold his sword of office on ceremonial occasions.

Instructions were also given to Wayo on good governance and how to behave and speak well in public. Here, the kingmakers placed more emphasis on settling of cases because he was not only going to be a chief but also a judge and he had to settle different kinds of cases. So they prayed to God to grant him Solomon's wisdom and fairness in judging cases in order to obtain the favor of the people.

Other things he was instructed in included how to dance to tune of the palace music, obonu. It is performed on all royal occasions by all-male drummers and singers, accompanied by a chorus of both sexes. The format of dancing is just like that of any war dance and so it was done in a more vigorous way. If a chief had to dance to the tune of obonu music, he could do it with the option of holding his sword or without it.

During ceremonial occasions, he had to sit in a palanquin with a little boy, his "kla" (soul) in front of him, and be carried to the ceremonial ground. And so he was given instructions in this palanquin ride and how to acknowledge greetings from his admirers. Finally, he was instructed on the dos and don'ts of a chief. One of these things was that a chief was not to eat in public. The concern was not necessarily with the eating but with the one who cooked the food. Anything cooked by a woman in her menstrual period was not to be eaten by a chief. It was believed that the eating of such food defiled the stool and its occupant, chief. And so since one could not be sure who did the cooking during a public occasion, the ancestors ruled that chiefs should not eat in public at all, as a precaution.

The actual ritual of Wayo's installation was performed on the seventh day. A very fat white sheep was slaughtered and its blood was allowed to drop onto Wayo's feet. A kingmaker then poured libation, saying:

'Tswa, tswa manye aba.' (May good tidings come to us.)

'Hia o,' (Amen) responded the others.

As the kingmaker poured the schnapps down in little bits for the second and third time, he chanted the accompanying prayers again:

'Tswa, tswa manye aba.'

'Hia o'

'Our God in heaven, our gods and ancestors of the land and rivers of Adoma,' the kingmaker continued, 'our son, Wayo, has returned home and we are today installing him as our new chief.'

'Hia o.' (Amen)

'We implore you to give him good health.'

'Hia o.'

'Give him wisdom and courage.'

'Hia o.'

After pouring down the last drop of the schnapps, two kingmakers held Wayo by the arm close to his shoulders and symbolically placed him on the stool two times. On the third occasion, he was left on the stool. Then his symbols of office were presented. These included a golden sword, two pairs of native sandals, two pieces of traditional cloth and a horse-tail. Libation was poured again to ask for more blessings for Wayo, now Chief Nene Tsatsu 111. After this, he was presented to the chief kingmaker on whose laps he was asked to sit for a while, amidst a thunderous applause from the onlookers.

Before he was made chief, Wayo was told that he would be given a stool wife. A stool wife was a traditional wife that was given to a chief on his installation. That would mean having two wives because he already had a wife. But he objected to it vehemently. He told the kingmakers he was already married and, as a Christian, it would be against the teachings of his religion. But the kingmakers were adamant. They would not accept the reasons he gave them. They explained to him that a stool wife was necessary and that everything had to be done according to the established tradition. Still Wayo would not yield and so the kingmakers suspended the discussion of the stool wife, hoping that when the time came for the marriage ceremony to be performed, he would understand the importance of such a wife. Wayo became relieved. He thought that was the end of the stool wife matter.

But that was not the end. The duty of the elders would not be complete without Nene Tsatsu's marriage to a stool wife. So the kingmakers had to perform this traditional ceremony by all means. When the matter came up again, Nene Tsatsu was as steadfast in his opposition to the idea as he was when he was first told about it. He did not want a second wife.

So the battle line between the two ideological groups was drawn. On one side were the kingmakers who wanted to adhere to established traditional norms and marry the chief to a stool wife. On the other side was the chief who did not want a stool wife because that would be against religious principles. So he threatened that if the elders continued to insist on a second wife, then he would relinquish the stool.

This argument dragged on for a long time without a compromise. The kingmakers knew Nene Tsatsu could not easily vacate the office, and so they did not take his threat seriously. All the same, they did not want to force him into the marriage. They wanted all the traditional rites to be done with an understanding and in a peaceful atmosphere.

Therefore they decided to involve Nene Tsatsu's family members in the negotiation to break the impasse. Three influential members of the family were therefore invited to the palace to help explain to the chief the necessity of a stool wife, and to let him know that it was unavoidable. Even with the presence of his relatives, it was difficult for the chief to accept what he was being asked to do. It took a long time of persuasion before eventually he changed his mind and gave his consent to the marriage. That was a tremendous relief to everybody.

The next day, Abla, who had already been earmarked by the kingmakers, was married to Nene Tsatsu amidst pomp and pageantry. The traditional Obonu and klama musical groups were in attendance to provide the necessary music and dance on the occasion. The celebration and the merry-making after the marriage ceremony lasted the whole day and into the night.

The following week, a Traditional Council of seven members was formed. Nanor was unanimously chosen as the chief's Linguist, spokesman and leader. Kingmakers Huno and Okete were endorsed as council members because of their vast experience in chieftaincy matters and the role they played in bringing Wayo home for installation. Also in the team was Kwao, a level-headed and well respected elder from the royal family of Nene Tsatsu. The rest included Akortorku and Goku, representing the other royal family, and Akutey, the elder kingmaker.

All the members were honorable men, well known and respected in the village. Huno and Okete had been kingmakers for years. They gained their respect from their honesty and charity work. As kingmakers, they never influenced the choice of candidates. On one occasion, Huno had to stand in as the chief when there was an impasse in the choice of a candidate. Okete, the other kingmaker, played a major role in Wayo's home coming. He was good at public relations and so he used his experience in persuading Wayo's mother and family to give their consent to the installation, and blessings to Wayo.

Everybody was satisfied with the composition of the council and so preparations started for chief Nene Tsatsu's presentation to the general public. His family members were contacted and the presentation was scheduled for the following month. A committee was then formed to make arrangements for the ceremony and the invitation of neighboring chiefs and local council officials.

Chapter 3

The day Nene Tsatsu 111 was presented to the general public; the village was so filled to capacity that it almost got burst. As early as seven o'clock in the morning, people from the neighboring villages and towns started converging on Adoma. Nene Tsatsu was the first educated person to be made chief in the whole district and this fact, coupled with the circumstances surrounding his installation as chief of Adoma, made people want to see him and participate in his presentation ceremony. Excitement was therefore very high.

The various traditional musical groups were in attendance. The first to arrive was the Oglodjo group led by Alu, nicknamed Gramophone. He got this name because of the melodious way he used to sing. Whenever he sang, his voice always produced different musical tones to the delight of listeners. On four consecutive occasions, Gramophone won the best traditional musical group leader award in the whole district. After his last award, he cut down his public appearances. He appeared only on very important occasions and so many people were eager to hear him sing on this august occasion.

Next to arrive was the Obonu group, led by Wetse, the antelope. He was famous for his dexterous dancing. In spite of his tiny legs, Antelope could dance so fast and indulge in heart-rending antics which always marveled people. He danced as if his legs did not touch the ground, and people even believed that that was true. Obonu was court music and so its members were very versed in traditional matters as well as war dances.

The all-women Klama group followed the Obonu musicians. It was led by Awo. Unlike the Oglodjo and Obonu groups which appeared on both sad and joyous occasions, the Klama musicians appeared mainly on happy occasions. They were therefore associated with initiation, marriage or wedding ceremonies or social events.

The Asafo and the Hunters groups were not left out. They came in their colorful war dresses, singing war songs and dancing to them. Their leader, Akaa, attracted the most attention. He was short and had a protruding pot-belly. But, in spite of his size, he could plant the blade of his sword in the ground with his right hand, throw his legs in the air and spin on the handle of the sword, to the amazement of onlookers. He was one of the warriors who fought in the Kabo wars and was instrumental in the victory of the Kabos which cleared the way for them to descend the hills and sojourn on the plains. It was during the wars, it was said, that he acquired his magical powers.

By half past eight, all nooks and corners of the Laasi, the ceremonial ground was occupied, except for the places reserved for invited chiefs and guests. One could not hear anything apart from the music emanating from the various musical groups which filled the whole atmosphere. When the chiefs started arriving, the music heightened into a crescendo. Their arrival added more pomp and pageantry to the occasion. Dressed in colorful traditional kente cloths and swords in their right hands, they sat in padded palanquins decorated with colorful buntings.

In front of each chief sat his kla. A chief's soul was normally a small boy of the court who always accompanied the chief on ceremonial occasions. The chief of Trawa was the last to arrive before Nene Tsatsu 111. When people got to know that Nene Lomo was coming, there was great anxiety and movement. Everybody wanted to have a glimpse of him. But they could not get closer because movement was impossible. All that people could do was to move their bodies forward and backward on their still legs.

Nene Lomo arrived in a palanquin carried by six people unlike the others who were carried by four people. He was dressed in a flamboyant kente cloth and was waving his sword to acknowledge greetings from the people. Occasionally, Nene Lomo would stand up in the palanquin and dance gracefully. That was characteristic of him. He was never afraid of tumbling down and breaking his neck. It was said that he acquired juju powers during the wars which enabled him to perform different kinds of stunts. During the Kabo wars, for example, it was said he was able to vanish and reappear unsuspectingly behind enemy lines.

People cheered and yelled when Nene Lomo arrived at the ceremonial ground. He was taken round in his palanquin to greet the people and the other chiefs who were already seated. When he took his seat, the other chiefs too, in turns, went to him to reciprocate his greetings. As this formality was going on, there were shouts of: 'Emaaoo! Nene maa oo!

'Awo o Awo!' He is coming, Nene is coming! Man born on Thursday, filled the whole atmosphere. These were the chants that heralded the arrival of Nene Tsatsu 111, and they were repeated several times.

Nene Tsatsu was carried in a simple but exquisite palanquin. He was clad in rich white kente cloth, just as his soul who sat in front of him. In his hair was a bunch of ostrich feathers. The executioners, dressed in their war attires led the way. On either side of the chief were the praise-singers, mostly women in jubilant mood. Occasionally, they cried out and chanted:

'Emaaoo! Nene maa oo!' This chant was always followed by the traditional response:

'Awo o Awo!'

Nene Tsatsu's reception at the Laasi ceremonial ground was more tumultuous than that given to chief Lomo. The anxiety was very strong, the yells were more thunderous and the chanting more deafening. At a certain stage, it looked as if the whole ground was moving toward Nene Tsatsu. At this time, it was not only the women who were singing. Almost everybody took over the chorus as soon as the praise-singers started the chant.

The new chief was taken round to greet his people and the invited guests. Among them were representatives of the United Africa Company where Nene Tsatsu 111 used to work. When he took his seat, the other chiefs and the invited guests, in turn, went to pay homage to him. Once a while, a praise-singer would punctuate the music still going on with a chant. This would be picked up and repeated by the teeming people.

When the chiefs and the invited guests had gone back to their seats, Nanor, the linguist, mounted the dais. On his left and right, he could see a multitude of jubilant people, and in front of him, the state umbrellas over the heads of the chiefs and the invited guests which seemed to have been woven together to form a canopy.

Nanor surveyed his audience and cried for silence: 'Ago o o o! Ago o o! Your attention, please!'

But nobody paid attention to his request for silence. The music still went on as if nothing had been said. Nanor repeated his appeal for silence but again the drums continued to beat, and the intoxicated singers and dancers still danced like mad. It was after the third appeal that the music faded into silence and the ground became quiet. Nanor surveyed his audience again and began to speak:

'Nene me (chiefs here present), Okyeame (Linguists), elders, our invited guests, brothers and sisters: On behalf of the people of Adoma, I welcome you all to the presentation of our new chief, Nene Tsatsu 111.'

This was followed by the usual enthusiastic and jubilant praise chants. Nanor gave the singers time to show their joy and then continued his speech. He spoke at length about the innovation which the people of Adoma had brought in the choice of chiefs; with particular reference to Nene Tsatsu, and paid a glowing tribute to the new chief for accepting to be the first chief of the innovation. Then he implored the Lord to grant him wisdom and courage; and the people, cooperation and constructive criticism so that Nene Tsatsu could be the chief they wanted him to be.

Then Nanor formally introduced Chief Nene Tsatsu 111 to the other chiefs, the invited guests and all the people present amidst shouts of joy and praise singing. This was followed immediately by the swearing in ceremony which was done by three elders of Adoma. All of them assured Nene Tsatsu that they would always be by him. Speaking separately, the first elder swore by his honor that he would be loyal to him and hoped that all the people of Adoma too would give him the necessary support to enable him discharge his duties. The second elder promised the chief that he would never fail to honor his call whenever it was made, whether in tribulation or in peace. In his promise to the chief, the third elder assured him that whenever he called him, whether in rain or in shine, he would respond immediately.

In his response, Nene Tsatsu thanked the elders and all the people of Adoma for the trust they had in him. He promised that with their cooperation, he would fearlessly lead them to realize their hopes and aspirations. Adoma needed to be developed, he told them, and in order to have the developments they needed, there were many things they could do by themselves instead of waiting for government. Then without going into details he announced that he had many achievable plans for the development he was talking about, and hoped that everybody would rally behind him to execute his plans. He promised to work together with the other chiefs and all government agencies to make the development of the village possible.

After Nene Tsatsu 111's speech, homage was paid to him by the other chiefs and some of the invited guests. The Personnel Manager of United Africa Company congratulated him on his being crowned chief of Adoma. He told him he was particularly pleased with his desire to help develop Adoma and assured him that if there was anything his Company could do to help him in his developmental plans, he would gladly advise his Company to do so. Turning to the people of Adoma, he advised them to be steadfast in their support for their chief because he had the greatest confidence in him. For many years, he told them, he had worked with him and had known him to be a selfless and hardworking man.

Nene Lomo, speaking on behalf of all the chiefs, also congratulated Nene Tsatsu on his installation. In his short speech, he recounted his past experiences and advised Nene Tsatsu to stand firm by what he believed in and be impartial in all his dealings with his people. It is by doing that, he told the new chief, that he would get the necessary support from all in discharging his duties. At the end of his speech, he presented a gift to Nene Tsatsu. This was followed by other gifts from the rest of the chiefs and some of the invited guests. They included live sheep, foodstuffs, native sandals and kente cloths. The representative of his former employer presented four pieces of Dumas cloths and two pairs of native sandals.

The musical groups became very busy after the presentations when the merry making actually started.

Everywhere, one could see people dancing to the various musical groups in action. Many of the chiefs danced too, but they danced only to the Obonu music, in turns. The ecstasy was unimaginable. When Nene Tsatsu entered the floor, the music heightened and people moved closer to have a glimpse of him. As an educated person who spent most of his life with the white people, they obviously wanted to find out how well he could dance to the traditional

42

music. But contrary to their expectation, Nene Tsatsu 111 surprised all of them. He danced to the amazement and admiration of everybody. The chants, praise-singing and the applause that accompanied his dancing display could be heard far and wide.

While the merry-making was going on, the cooking of the fat cow which was slaughtered earlier on was complete. This was served to the people with cooked yam or rice which gave them more energy to dance into the evening.

A week, later, Nene Tsatsu was presented to Nene Obuaba, the paramount chief of the district. A paramount chief, according to tradition, did not attend a formal introductory ceremony of new chiefs. Instead, he waited in his palace for the new chief to be presented to him. On this occasion, the crowd was not very large. Nene Tsatsu was followed only by his elders and a few praise-singers who waved small branches of trees in their hands as they praise sang. These women praise-singers walked faster ahead of the chief and so reached the palace first. But they did not get in. They walked back immediately to the chief and escorted him to Obuaba's residence.

Nene Tsatsu was warmly received by the palace officials and after the traditional greetings; he was officially introduced and presented to Nene Obuaba. This was followed by the swearing of allegiance. Nene Tsatsu 111 swore to the paramount chief that he would always be loyal to him, adhere to the traditional norms and practices of their ancestors, and abide by all rules and decisions taken by the Traditional Council. In welcoming him, Nene Obuaba advised Nene Tsatsu to be fair but firm in everything he wanted to do for his people, and be sure that his elders were always behind him. Then he presented his new chief with many kinds of gifts, including a golden neck lace. This was followed by Klama music and dance by the women praise-singers which lasted for a long time.

At the end of the day back to his own palace, Nene Tsatsu revisited all the events leading to his coming back to the village and his installation as chief of Adoma. He thought over the drama that unfolded in the city which culminated in his being brought to the village, the traditional norms he had to go through and his installation. Even though he did not regret his uncooperative attitudes toward the elders in the city, he felt the call was a legitimate service to his people. So he resigned himself to doing the best he could to satisfy the aims and aspirations of the people. Then he prayed to God to give him peace and wisdom to enable him attain the wishes of his people.

Chapter 4

Nene Tsatsu spent the next few days in the palace receiving visitors and well-wishers. They came either to congratulate him on his installation, or pay homage and present gifts to him. The first to call was the chief's mother who had not been seen since the incident preceding her son's coronation. She came with presents of various kinds to wish him well. Her visit was a gigantic relief to many people especially the kingmakers who saw it as a sign of reconciliation with the chieftaincy, and a blessing to the chief.

Later in the day, other visitors followed. They included Nene Tsatsu's city friend, Saki, and a delegation from the U.A.C., headed by the Personnel Manager. After the normal customary greetings, four bottles of schnapps were presented to the visitors for the traditional leg-washing ceremony. Since chiefs did not pour libation, Okyeame Nanor got up, moved forward and lowered his cloth to his waist. A glass was given to him into which was poured some of the schnapps. He bent forward and as he poured the drink down in little bits, he prayed:

'Nene Mau nge hiowe ke yozugbazu, nye ba nu.' (Our God in heaven and Mother Earth, come and drink with us.)

As he prayed, the elders and attendants responded:

'Hia o.' (Amen)

'The gods of our rivers and hills, who always see that we get food and water to drink, come and drink with us.'

'Hia o.'

'Our ancestors and who have protected us over the years come and drink with us.'

'Amen.'

'We thank you for the life you have put into us and for bringing our august visitors safely to this place.'

'Amen.'

'We hope their visit will be fruitful and at the end you will guide them safely back to the city.'

'Hia o!'

'Tswa, tswa, tswa manye aba!' (May prosperity come to us.)

'Hia o!'

On the last prayer, Okyeame Nanor poured the rest of the drink on the ground and returned to his seat. He was served with the drink again but this time he drank it. Then the rest of the people were all served. When everybody had had something to drink, the chief informed his visitors, through his linguist, that everything at home was peaceful and that he was ready to hear them.

The Manager apologized to Nene Tsatsu for his inability to attend his crowning ceremony. He explained that the date coincided with an appointment he had already accepted. Then in congratulating the chief, he said:

'We are here today on behalf of United Africa Company, the Company you faithfully served for eight years, to rejoice with you in your new role and to wish you the best of luck in discharging your duties.'

'We thank you all for your coming,' responded Nene Tsatsu.

'In appreciation of your meritorious services to the Company,' the Manager continued, 'we wish to present to you on behalf of the Company, the following presents:'

A man got up, opened a box and brought out the following: four pieces of Dumas cloths (wax prints), two pieces of native kente cloths, two pairs of sandals, a dozen bottles of schnapps, and cash gift of five hundred pounds.

Okyeame Nanor received the presents on behalf of Nene Tsatsu and expressed his sincere gratitude to the visitors and the Company as a whole for the amazing presents. The Manager then assured his former Assistant Personnel Manager that his entitlements would be paid in full and that as soon as they were ready, he would be notified.

In response to the Manager's speech, Nene Tsatsu 111 expressed his profound thanks to his visitors and his former Company for the honor they had done to him. Then according to tradition, he asked his linguist to serve the four bottles of the schnapps they brought to all the people. This was followed by friendly discussions after which the visitors bade farewell to the chief.

By this time, the palace was almost full of inquisitive onlookers. News of the presence of the visitors from the city spread quickly and people, mostly children, started converging on the palace just to have a glimpse of the white people among them. The increasing number of these intruders was becoming so embarrassing that one of the elders advised the gateman not to allow anybody into the yard anymore.

The visitors were amazed to find so many people around when they got out of the palace. And when they got to know from Saki the actual reason why they were there, the Manager asked:

'You mean they are here just to look at us?'

'Yes. You see many of them have not seen a white person at a close range before.'

'That is interesting.' The Manager remarked.

The curious children followed the visitors all the way to the extreme end of the village. They did not mind walking back once their curiosity was satisfied.

The meeting with the visitors from the city was the last unofficial business Nene Tsatsu did after his installation. Two days after this meeting, he began his official chieftaincy duties with a meeting with his council of elders. He thanked them for the various roles they played before, and during his installation and presentation ceremonies.

'Some of you must be wondering,' he continued, 'whether I have wholeheartedly accepted the stool. To allay your fears,' he went on, 'I wish to say that I have. All that I need now is your cooperation and guidance.'

There was a tremendous prolonged applause at the end of which Nanor happily remarked:

'I am extremely elated to hear this assurance from Nene. Those who are going about saying that we have wrongly made you a chief should come and listen.' Adoma is my village,' Nene Tsatsu continued. 'I was born and bred here, and so this place is my home. It was only business which made me leave for the city.'

'Then why didn't you quickly accept the invitation to come home to occupy the stool?' interjected Akortorku.

The elders glanced at each other with disapproval for a few seconds and then Kwao responded to his question:

'You see,' he continued, 'it is not easy to leave a promising job for another one you do not know much about. Therefore Nene needed time to make up his mind. So when we were chasing him up and down in Accra, I was not worried. Even when mosquitoes were biting me and feeding on me, I didn't complain,' Kwao concluded in a joke.

There was prolonged laughter from everybody on hearing the word "mosquitoes". Many people, even those who had not been to the city before knew how deadly mosquitoes were in Accra, and those who were in the three royal delegations could testify to that. Since laughing is contagious, Nene Tsatsu could not help laughing too.

When the laughing stopped, he made things clear to everybody. He made them understand that it was not the coming back to settle in the village or the fear of the stool that he was worried about. He was concerned, he went on, about the people of Adoma and unsure whether he would get the necessary support to discharge his duties. In many places, he told the elders, chiefs did not get the cooperation they needed to do their work efficiently. And as a result of that, they always became frustrated and unable to achieve their aims.

Nene Tsatsu therefore hoped that would not happen in Adoma and that together, they would be able to transform their village into a town. On the other hand, he warned, if they allowed rumor-mongering and litigation to permeate their minds nothing could be achieved. Even though he was their chief, he asked them not to consider him as a deity because he was to serve Adoma and not to lord over the

49

people. Anybody could come and share ideas with him any time, but he warned against coming to him without any genuine business in mind.

He told his councilors their priority was the development of their village which they could start without necessarily waiting for government. 'Government cannot do everything for all the country,' he said. Then he put his development plans before his councilors. They included the rehabilitation of the feeder road leading to the market at Kesua and the outside world, a permanent building for the only primary school they had, and a clinic where sick people could easily be treated instead of carrying them all the way to the clinic at Kesua.

'We cannot allow our women and children to be carrying foodstuffs on their fragile heads, six miles away, all the time,' Nene Tsatsu continued. 'Therefore,' he went on, 'if we are able to complete the construction of the road, many drivers would be pleased to bring their vehicles here to convey our foodstuffs to the market. At the moment, I hear some of our school children sit under trees to be taught; which means when there is bad weather, there are no classes. We can stop this by putting up a school block for them.' While the councilors were expressing their approval for the plans Nene Tsatsu was laying down before them, Akortorku got up and cloaked:

'I have something to say, Nene.'

'Go on, we need more ideas,' responded the chief.

'We tried several times to complete the road but the Koro hill always posed a threat to us because of its steep and rocky nature,' said Akortorku.

'There is a solution to that. We shall divert the road eastward where there is a more gradual slope.'

'That will bring another problem, Nene. It will mean many acres of people's farms; cocoa farms in particular, will be destroyed.'

'Yes, in the interest of Adoma,' Nene Tsatsu retorted. 'In this world,' he went on, 'some people have to suffer the loss of some things or even sacrifice their lives for the sake of others.' Then quoting the bible, he told them that Jesus Christ sacrificed his own life to save the whole world from sin. He also reminded them of how many of their people died in the Koro wars to save Adoma. Therefore he did not think it was too much for people to sacrifice portions of their farms for a road to be constructed to save their women from carrying goods on their heads to the market at Kesua. Then he appealed to all those who might be affected by the diversion for their cooperation.

Huno then spoke in support of Nene, laying emphasis on the benefits of the road when completed. 'In addition to what Nene had already been said,' he went on:

'It will open Adoma to the outside world and help in our development. We must therefore not allow personal interests to…'

'What do you mean by personal interest?' Akortorku broke protocol. 'Is there anybody here whose actions are not motivated by vested interest? We are talking about people's farms on which their lives depend.'

'My farm will be affected, too, Akortorku,' Okete intervened. 'But I will not mind if a few of my cocoa trees are razed to make way for the road,' Okete continued.

Nene Tsatsu did not want the meeting to degenerate into confrontation. So he appealed to members to respect the stool and stop the war-cloud. When sanity was restored, he stressed that the road had to be constructed by all means. So he advised all those who were likely to lose parts of their farms to be considerate and cooperative. He reminded members of what happened in the week when a woman in labor had to deliver on the way to Kesua, and lost the child. If the road were motor able, this woman would have been taken to hospital quickly, and the child could have been saved.

Nanor suggested that the diversion of the road should be put into a vote. And when this was done, the result was unanimous in favor of the diversion to go ahead. The chief then made all members aware that all the projects would be executed through communal labor and he appealed to members to go out and educate the people on them. Before the meeting ended, committees were appointed to make the necessary arrangements for the start of work, beginning with the road.

On his way back home, Nanor fell into the company of Akortorku and Okete. The three reviewed their first meeting with their chief and Nanor's estimation of him was that he had ideas that could be used to bring progress to their village. Okete agreed with him, adding that the chief showed that he had great concern for the people of Adoma.

'What concern for the people?' Akortorku responded. 'What kind of concern?' he repeated. 'He just wanted to create the impression that he knows better than all of us. This is what the so-called educated people think. How many times did we not try to complete the road and failed because of the insurmountable problems that faced us?'

'It was because we were not seriously united then.' Nanor reacted.

'And how can you be sure that this time we are, and that the problems will not be there?'

'We all agreed with Nene to divert the road to make the work easier. It is the right thing to do in this situation, Akortorku.'

'You can say what you like but when one's source of livelihood is at stake, he has to fight.'

'What do you mean by that, Akortorku? Is it the diversion of the road you are talking about?' asked Okete who had been quiet all the time.

'Yes, of course. You all know that I am the only one whose farm will suffer the most. That's why you supported the idea.'

'You are wrong,' Nanor interposed. 'The western side of the hill is so steep and thick-forested that we cannot continue to waste our time there again. You have to understand the situation.'

'And so I should sacrifice my farm. No. If you want to complete the road so that your friends in the city can come to visit you in their cars, you don't have to destroy my farm.

'The road is not being constructed because of Nene and surely not because of visitors, Nanor corrected him.

In his further defense of Nene Tsatsu, he told Akortorku that their chief had genuine plans for the village which needed the support of everybody. He did not have time to respond to what Nanor said because he had to make a turn to his house.

53

Okete and Nanor were very unhappy about Akortorku's utterances. Okete stated that the Koro hill was no more a problem to them and that the real problem was he. Nanor agreed with him but he was optimistic that his opposition would not stop the diversion of the road which had to be constructed. He prayed that the majority of the elders who voted in favor of diversion would continue to have faith in Nene Tsatsu. With this, they parted.

Chapter 5

The palace messenger went to all parts of the village to invite the general public to a meeting which the chief scheduled for five o'clock the following day. He beat his gong three times to announce his presence before giving his message; and another three times to conclude. That was traditional. As soon as people heard of the beatings of a gong, they knew there was a message coming from the palace.

A great number of people turned up for the meeting at Laasi Park. Among those who were conspicuously absent was Akortorku. To Nanor and Okete, that was not unexpected considering his utterances during their discussion on their way home after the meeting with the chief. Nene Tsatsu 111 arrived on schedule, this time, without much fanfare. He was only accompanied by members of his council and a few women praise-singers. The only thing that identified him was the state umbrella over him. The carrier, as usual, held it high above the chief and occasionally made it turn in a spinning motion, or raised it up and down over the chief's head as they walked along.

After a short introductory speech by Linguist Nanor, Nene Tsatsu started to speak. This time the women praise-singers could not help keeping quiet. They spontaneously burst into chanting: 'Awo o Awo!' He gave them time to finish their chant and then continued.

'My fathers, mothers, brothers and sisters;' he went on, 'I thank you so much for coming to this very important meeting. Before I talk about the purpose for which I have called you here, I wish to thank you again for the confidence you have in me and for the cooperation you have given me so far. You...' A woman punctuated his speech with a praise chant. 'You will agree with me,' he went on, 'that Adoma is one of the least developed villages in the whole Kesua district. It has no good social amenities to make people live here happily. Some of our school children still sit under trees or sheds to be taught and are always at the mercy of the sun or rain. We trek six miles to Kesua to sell our foodstuffs and to buy the things we need.'

'Adoma needs to be developed to make life better for us and if the government is unable to provide us with the amenities we need, then we have to do the things we can do to change our lives. I met with my council members and we decided on some projects which we can undertake to bring some progress to Adoma. But we cannot embark on the projects we have ear-marked without the knowledge and full participation of you all. This is the reason why I have called you here. Okyeame Nanor will now tell you more about the developmental projects.'

When the long applause that followed Nene Tsatau's speech ended, Nanor threw more light on the projects to be embarked upon. They included the rehabilitation of the feeder road to Kesua, the building of a permanent classroom block and a clinic.

The acclamation that followed was long and reassuring.

'Now that you have given us your approval,' he continued, 'we know that our aims will be achieved. Very soon, the rains will be our uninvited guests and our children will start suffering again. We do not want to allow this to continue to happen and so we shall start our projects with the building of the school block.' There was a long applause again after which a woman in the crowd exclaimed: 'We now have a chief!'

Nanor then told the people about detailed arrangements for work to start.

'Saturdays and Wednesdays are our markets days,' he reminded them. 'While our women are gone to the market, we the men will be working on the school building and any other project that will follow. The only people who will be exempted are children, the aged and the sick.'

In an answer to a question as to when work would start, Nanor informed the people work on the school block would begin the next market day, which was Wednesday. Then he asked them to bring along working implements such as cutlasses, hoes, pick-axes, shovels, wheel-barrows, large bowls or anything they would consider useful. With regard to materials, he informed the people that Nene Tsatsu had made arrangements for the supply of cement and corrugated roofing sheets from the city.

Questions were asked and a few issues were raised but all were satisfactorily addressed. With reference to the diversion of the road which some people were concerned about, Nanor explained that that was the only possible way construction work could be done because of the steep and stony hill. He assured everybody that only the necessary cocoa trees would be destroyed to make way for the road.

On their way back home and at home, people discussed both the intended projects and their chief. To most of them, Nene Tsatsu sounded like one who would not only sit in the comfort of the palace, receiving visitors and drinking schnapps. They wanted a chief who would be concerned about their needs and work hard to bring progress to Adoma. That chief, to them, was Nene Tsatsu 111.

Akortorku spent the whole day sleeping since it was a market day and he did not have to go to the farm to do any serious work. In the evening, he went to sit down on a bench under a huge neem-tree in front of his house, puffing his pipe. At that time, people were then passing by, on their way to their various homes. Many of them greeted him but none said anything about the meeting with the people.

Goku would have passed too without saying anything either with reference to the meeting. But Akortorku engaged him in a conversation when he greeted him:

'The meeting was a useful one. Many people were present. Why were you not there?'

'Me? You do not know what is happening.'

'No. Is there anything going on?'

'You cannot read people's minds,' Akortorku responded. 'Is it not our turn to supply a candidate for the stool this time?'

'Yes. But it was a general agreement to have an educated person and since—'

'Haven't we had illiterate chiefs over the years and didn't they perform well?' Akortorku cut in. 'It was a plan to deprive us of our right if you do not know.'

'But the advantages of a chief who can read and write were discussed and all of us supported the choice of Wayo.'

'No, I didn't because I knew it was a conspiracy. Don't you know that Nanor who spear-headed the nomination is a relative of Wayo. We can still show our displeasure,' he went on, 'by boycotting the chief and fighting for what should be ours.'

By this time, darkness had almost enveloped the whole village. So Goku took leave of him. He pondered over Akortorku's grievances. It was true that the present chief should have come from his family but he was a party to the change in the selection process. He agreed to the innovation and so, personally, he did not think there was any need to complain or reject the new chief.

Meanwhile, feverish arrangements for the start of work on the school building continued. On the second day after the meeting, Nene Tsatsu left for the city, his first after his installation. At U.A.C, his former colleagues were delighted to see him again. The workers hailed and addressed him by his rightful title, Nene. He was no more Mr. Wayo as they used to call him. The Personnel Manager was happy his Company had produced a chief for the people of Adoma.

From the U.A.C., he visited the Ministry of Education and Rural Development. At these two places, the chief had discussions with the officials concerned about the projects he wanted to embark upon at Adoma and appealed for support. And he was not disappointed. The U. A. C. promised to supply cement and corrugated iron roofing sheets. The Education Ministry officials also promised materials and technical assistance for which Nene Tsatsu was hugely grateful. All these promises and assurances were in addition to others from the chief's personal friends. The work on the school building was therefore set to begin. It did not take very long when the materials started arriving. Since the road was not motor able to Adoma, a depot was established at Sonson from where the materials were manually carried to the village.

The first few working days were used to clear the site and put things in order. While some of the people were doing this, others were bringing some of the materials from Sonson. It could be seen from the high turn out that the people had embraced the spirit of self-help projects which they hoped would bring progress to their village. They showed this spirit by their enthusiasm and preparedness to work.

Nene Tsatsu broke tradition and led the way. Whenever he had no official duties to perform at the palace, he went to the site and actually participated in the work. His continuous presence at the work site marveled many people, and soon he became a topic of discussion. To the traditionalists, their chief's action was a taboo. They condemned his condescension to work with the people. As a chief, they argued, his noble status had to be maintained. He had to restrict himself to palace duties only.

The modernizers viewed their chief in a different perspective. They argued that Nene Tsatsu was not only a chief but also a leader and, as a leader, they saw nothing wrong with his involvement in community work. Good leaders, they stressed, always set examples and that was just what their chief was doing. Nene Tsatsu was aware of the debate going on about him but he paid no attention to it. He combined his official duties with taking part in the community projects and working on his personal farms. His chieftaincy duties included the performance of the traditional rituals as they were laid down by the ancestors, settling of petty squabbles, family problems, land disputes and sometimes criminal cases, like rape. Normally on Tuesdays, he worked on his personal farms.

One Tuesday morning, Akortorku decided to go to the palace knowing very well that Nene Tsatsu would not be there. When he got there, he asked Naki:

'Is the chief in?'

'No, he is gone to the farm,' she replied.

Naki saw that Akortorku was unhappy and so she asked him if there was anything wrong. He responded in the negative and left unceremoniously. On his way back home, he stopped at Okete's residence. He was just about to leave for his carpentry workshop when he got there. Okete was a famous carpenter at Adoma and its environs. Carpentry was a family profession that was handed over to him.

But unlike his predecessors, he did not depend solely on this work. He married carpentry with farming which was then a major occupation in Adoma. A man's wealth and reputation depended on the number of barns of yams or corn that he had. So he did his farm work conscientiously. But he had time, too, to make the benches, tables, bedsteads and the coffins when they were needed.

No sooner had Akortorku sat down than he started complaining about Nene Tsatsu:

'I am from the palace,' he informed Okete.

'I see. How is the chief?'

'How is he? I didn't even meet him. I was told he had gone to the farm. I don't know what kind of a chief he is,

Okete. He is always either gone to the city or to the farm. Have we made him a chief or a farmer?'

'Akortorku, Nene has to eat and you know we cannot feed him and his family all the time.' What we give him is not even enough.'

'What are you talking about? We have a chief who will not stay in the palace and you are saying he has to eat.'

'Ah! Well.'

'If he is not on his personal farm, he is building a school or gone to the city. Meanwhile, the Stool is left unoccupied. Don't you think our ancestors will be cross with us?'

'You see, Akortorku, one thing I like about Nene is that he is extremely active. His attitudes are quite different from the ways of behavior of his predecessors.

'He wants to do things for himself and for the people. I don't think there is anything wrong with going to his farm, working with us on the projects or going to the city. In fact, we have gained a lot from his visits to the city. So let us give him the cooperation and the peace of mind to help us develop our village.' 'When it becomes evident that he his neglecting his main duties, then we shall have cause to complain.'

'There is enough evidence already.'

'I don't see it.'

Dissatisfied with Okete's responses, Akortorku left him. His ulterior motive was to play Okete against the chief, and gain his support. But he found him absolutely unbending. Already he had gained the support of Goku and some other prominent people in the village. But Okete was very important to him because he was a kingmaker. So he thought he could sway him to his side too, to secure more support for his opposition to Nene Tsatsu.

On his way home, Akortorku stopped at Huno's house thinking that he was at home. But Huno was not a man who would be at home at that time when the sun was high in the sky. When he got to his house, he took his cutlass and hoe and left for his farm. *Even if he could not do any appreciable work,* he thought, *he would get the chance to discuss matters with Huno.* Both of them shared a common boundary and so he was sure he would meet Huno on the farm. Akortorku reached the farm when his neighbor was having his afternoon break. He was amazed to see him coming to the farm at that time.

'Why, are you now coming?' Huno asked him.

'I had to go and check on an enterprise I am working on,' Akortorku replied. Then he went on, 'Now that you are resting, can we have some discussions?'

'Sure, sit down on that stone, please.' He took one of the fresh corns he was roasting and invited Akortorku to serve himself. After munching the corns for a while, he asked:

'How do you like how things are going on in the village now?'

'I can see signs of progress and we should be grateful to Nene Tsatsu. The school is almost completed and work on the rehabilitation of the road has started. Nene has awakened the consciousness of people, and everybody is anxious to work for the development of Adoma.'

'I am more concerned with his real traditional duties as a chief. He is most of the time out of the palace and when

63

people go there with their problems, he is not there to help them.'

'Nene has a schedule which he follows. You know he worked in the city before. Therefore...'

'I went round to sample people's opinion about him and the result was that a majority of the people are unhappy because he is not making himself an embodiment of our tradition.'

'That is debatable but this is not the place to discuss it. We are his councilors and if we see anything wrong, we should be bold enough to go to him and discuss it with him,' Huno retorted.

That was not the response Akortorku wanted but they had to end the dialogue and start work on their respective farms. Huno wanted to finish what he had ear-marked to do for the day before going back home.

Chapter 6

During the week, many people came to the palace to listen to a case brought to the traditional court. Earlier, Nene Tsatsu had a separate meeting with his councilors. At this meeting, issues concerning the on-going school project were discussed and plans for the start of the rehabilitation of the road were made. Before the meeting ended, the chief expressed his concern with Akortorku's constant absence from meetings and asked his councilors if any of them was in contact with him. At that stage, nobody was able to say anything but Nanor promised try to look for him.

When the court was convened, Nanor told the house that the case was against Opese and Damtey, and that it was brought by a concerned citizen of Adoma. The two men were alleged to have conspired to make money, and actually made money with the use of juju at the expense of people's health and ignorance. Then Nanor asked Osom, the plaintiff, to go ahead with his case.

In presenting his case, Osom told the court that for a long time, people had been suffering from one particular sickness. The rapidity with which they were getting sick, and then cured a few days later after paying a huge amount of money was a marvel to everybody. Therefore together with some concerned people, he decided to investigate the strange sickness. And from reliable sources, he got to know that the sickness was caused and cured by Opese and Damtey, with the power of juju.

When asked to describe the sickness, Osom explained:

'It is a strange sickness which attacks only men. It begins with waist pains and ends up making it difficult for one to bend down. Then the male organ shrivels and becomes hopelessly inactive.'

'Right, that's how it is. I had it for four days,' exclaimed an observer.

'Four days? Then you were lucky. I had it for seven days,' cried another observer.

At this stage, Nene Tsatsu reminded the people that they were in court and that nobody had the right to say anything unless asked to do so as a witness. He warned that anyone who contravened the rules of the court would be fined. Then he asked the councilors to continue with the case. Since then, nobody uttered a word for fear that he would be fined a live sheep.

'Tell us about your investigation.' Nanor asked.

'I got information from a number of people including some of the victims and a girl-friend of Damtey.'

'How do they inflict the sickness on people?' Huno inquired.

In his answer, Osom told the court that in their quest for quick money, Opese and Damtey travelled to a juju man in Damey. There they asked for a talisman which they could use to make money and so a juju pipe, together with a special tobacco, was sold to Opese. He was to smoke the tobacco and blow the smoke directly into a man's face and he would get the sickness which would last for a week. Damtey was asked to purchase a juju potion. The instruction was that within the week of a person contracting the sickness, he would go to him to cure him by rubbing the potion sold to him around his waist and he would be healed. But they were warned that the curing should be done within one week; otherwise the juju would lose its potency and the person would no more be free easily from the sickness.

When Opese and Damtey returned home, Osom went on, they made a list of people they considered too rich and made them their targets. So an itinerary was drawn which they followed. Opese went to people first to engage them in a conversation and while chatting, he would smoke his pipe and blow the smoke into the face of their target. A day or two afterward Damtey would go to the victims and through discussions tell them he had the power to heal them. Then he would use the potion the juju man sold to him to cure the sickness and free them from their predicament.

'So Opese goes first to make people sick and Damtey follows later to cure them. How then does making of money come in?' One of the councilors asked.

In an answer to the question, Osom told the court that before starting an operation, Opese and Damtey would agree to charge each victim an amount of fifty pounds for a cure. They always knew how many people they had inflicted the sickness on and cured each week. So at the end of the week, Opese and Damtey would meet and share their un-holy money.

At this stage, Nene Tsatsu asked Osom if he had witnesses who would corroborate his allegations. In his answer, Osom said he had three people to testify. The first to be called was Ajoa, Damtey's girlfriend. She told the court that she became very concerned when Damtey started giving her money more than she was getting before. She asked him where he was getting the extra money from and he initially refused to tell her the source of his income. But one day when he was drunk, he confided in her that he was using juju with Opese to make money.

The second witness was Nartey, a friend of Opese. He testified that he had known Opese as a non-smoker for a long time and so he was surprised to see him smoking a pipe one day. When he asked him when he started smoking, he replied that it was recently and that he smoked only occasionally. When people started getting sick after inhaling steam from his smoking, he became suspicious and started asking questions.

Kofi, one of the victims of the conspiracy was then called. He told the house that he had a chat with Opese one day, and got the sickness in the evening. Two days later, he met him again and when he got to know that he was sick, he advised him that he should not worry and that he knew someone who could restore his health. The following day, Damtey came to him and after rubbing some medicine around his waist, he became well the next day. Asked if he was charged any amount of money, Kofi told the court that Damtey demanded an amount of fifty pounds which he paid before his treatment.

Opese and Damtey were then called upon to present their version of the case. In their defense, they denied having any juju that could make people get sick. Opese told the court that his smoking had nothing to do with juju and that he was smoking to prevent him from getting tensed up all the times.

Damtey agreed that he could cure several types of sicknesses including waist pains but with traditional herbs and not with any mystical power. He described Ajoa's evidence as a frame-up, concocted to tarnish his reputation because of the strained cordiality between them. When asked whether they had ever travelled to Damey, Opese replied that they had been there several times to visit friends.

At this stage, Nene Tsatsu asked:

'Damtey, Ajoa said the money you are giving her now is more than she was getting previously yet you are not doing any visible extra work. Where are you getting that extra money from?'

'It is not extra money, Nene. I just decided to increase the money I was giving Ajoa because she was complaining that what I was giving her was not enough and I did not want her to leave me.'

Other members of the council also asked questions to clear their minds and then the court recessed to decide on the case. When it reconvened, it found Opese and Damtey guilty of indulging in juju to make illegal money. They were fined two hundred pounds, two live sheep and two bottles of the local gin popularly called akpeteshie, jointly. They were also ordered to refund the monies they collected from the people they made sick within a month. The victims were asked to report to the chief after the month if they had not got their monies back. In addition, Opese and Damtey were ordered to destroy the money-making charm they acquired and were warned that they would be ostracized if anybody got sick of that particular sickness again. As tradition demanded, one of the sheep was slaughtered and used as a sacrifice to cleanse the village and pacify all those who were made sick. Then in an advice before the court closed, Nene Tsatsu appealed to them to engage in decent jobs and referred them to the land, most of which was uncultivated.

The councilors had an extraordinary meeting with Nene Tsatsu soon afterward. It was at the instigation of Akortorku. Nene Tsatsu excused members and left them for a while. When he returned, Akortorku got up and started to speak:

'Nene, I know we have been sitting down here for a long time but I would like us to spend a few more minutes to discuss some vital issues.'

There were exchanges of glances from some of the members, especially those who were aware of the evil machinations of Akortorku. Nene Tsatsu adjusted himself in his seat innocently waiting to hear about the vital issues.

'As you said,' Nanor interposed, 'we have been here for a long time already and so try to be brief, Akortorku.'

'All right Nanor.' He then began to speak. 'Complaints I have received indicate that many people are dissatisfied with the way Nene is running the offices of the stool. I…'

'Dissatisfied?' Akutey, the elder kingmaker, asked in disbelief. Nene Tsatsu and many of the councilors were also shocked to hear Akortorku's allegation.

'Yes, many people are unhappy and they are complaining a lot,' he continued.

'What are they complaining about?' Nanor asked.

'The people are saying Nene is not occupying the stool as tradition demands. He does not maintain his status as a traditional chief, he does not concentrate on his traditional duties and he is always out of the palace. To them, Nene's behavior is an insult to the stool and a disgrace to the people of Adoma.' Akortorku concluded.

There was dead silence and many glances were exchanged again. Goku and Huno bent down their heads and so nothing could be read from their faces. Everybody thought Nene Tsatsu would react negatively. But he did not. That was not his nature. Rather, he shook his head, and then asked Akortorku:

'Did you previously discuss these allegations with any of the councilors?'

'Yes, Nene, many of them are aware of how the people feel,' Akortorku answered.

'I am not aware of anything,' Interjected Nanor.

'I know nobody is aware of anything because nothing is happening,' Nene Tsatsu nodded in his support and then he continued:

'All that Akortorku has said is his own contemptuous fabrication to undermine me. I knew something was happening. We had many meetings which he did not attend to let us know the grievances if there were any. And he did not even have the courtesy to let me know why he was unable to do so. So I can say now that he is the one who is trying to poison the minds of the people against me.'

'Me?' Akortorku sprang up. He looked round as if to appeal for support from his colleagues. But nobody uttered a word. They only looked at him in amazement. Even his accomplices could not say anything in support of him. Nene Tsatsu gave him time to react but he could not decide what to do under the circumstances and so he sat down.

'If what I am saying is not true, then you only have to deny it.' Nene Tsatsu advised him.

'What you are saying is not true, Nene.' Akortorku replied. 'I am not conspiring against you.' He continued.

'Yes, you are.' Nene Tsatsu insisted. 'But I am not going to quarrel with you,' he continued. Then addressing all his councilors, he went on:

'I wish to take this opportunity to ask all of you what you want me to do as your chief. Do you want me to be sitting down in the palace all the time, legs-crossed, only to be receiving sycophantic visitors? Would you then be feeding me and my family? By the way, how many of you have brought me foodstuffs since my coronation? Yet you do not want me to go out to work.'

Nene Tsatsu paused for a while. He deliberately stopped to allow what he was saying to impact on his councilors, and to listen to what any of them would say. But nobody was able to say anything. The hall continued to be as quite as a graveyard. One could even hear the sound of a falling dried leaf.

Since nobody wanted to say anything, Nene Tsatsu told his councilors that his position as a chief did not make him a demigod. So his duty was not to lord over the people but to serve and work with them in order to bring development to the village. In that regard, he had to work with and for the people. So he needed the cooperation of everyone, especially, they, his councilors. Nene Tsatsu then called his elders' attention to the materials and equipment they received for their projects and asked them how they could have got those things if he did not travel to the city to appeal for them. He, therefore, advised his councilors to educate the people to understand the actions they were taking to develop Adoma. He reminded them that it was only during biblical times that God fed the Israelites with manna from heaven. In these modern times, he went on; everybody had to work to feed himself. The world had changed and so everybody must change in perception and action to keep abreast with the changes, he advised.

When he asked his councilors if any of them would like to say anything, Nanor, who was unhappy with Akortorku's allegations, thanked Nene Tsatsu for all that he had said. He reassured him of their continued support, adding that if there were any clandestine activities against him, he personally did not think those involved were many.

Before the meeting came to an end, Nene Tsatsu reminded his councilors of the funeral rites of the late chief. It was a tradition to perform the final funeral ceremony of a late chief after a new one had been installed. A discussion was had and a date was scheduled. Three committees were formed to be in charge of the traditional rites, logistics and refreshment.

When Akortorku got home that day, he kept himself indoors. He spent the rest of the day and the whole night pondering over his actions. What he was doing was no more a secret so he decided to go ahead to achieve his aim. Then he thought of new plans to be executed to make his enterprise successful. Early in the morning, he went out to see Goku, Huno and some other key members in his group and a meeting was arranged. At this meeting, Akortorku moved and insisted on a total boycott of the chief and all his activities.

Most of his supporters were, however, not in support of an immediate break of relations with Nene Tsatsu because of the imminent funeral rites of the late chief. The general opinion was that the funeral was an obligation for all the people of Adoma to honor the late chief, and not Nene Tsatsu. A boycott would therefore displease the late chief and the gods, and the repercussion would be a curse on them. However, all of them agreed to continue with their campaign against the chief because they believed he was not doing what a real traditional chief should do.

On the day the conspirators met, Nanor went to visit the chief. On his way, he stopped at the chief's family house and informed his father about what transpired at their council meeting the previous day. Then he asked him to accompany him to the palace. After the necessary customary greetings, Nanor told Nene Tsatsu that he had come to register his personal apology to him for Akortorku's behavior at their last meeting. He acted as a disgruntled man and that was unfortunate and unacceptable but he hoped that Nene Tsatsu would not allow his diabolical activities to disturb him.

'Actually,' Nanor continued, 'I was disturbed because I was instrumental in your choice for the stool, and so I do not want people like him to give you unnecessary problems. This is the reason why I have asked your father to come with me to witness what I am coming to say.'

Nene Tsatsu accepted Nanor's apology, and asked him what he personally thought of Akortorku's allegations. This gave Nanor the opportunity to tell the chief all that he knew about him, beginning with what he said on the night they returned from the city. At the end, he assured the chief that a majority of the people of Adoma supported him and were in favor of his plans to develop the village. He had brought so much innovation in chieftaincy matters and developments taking to Adoma that only the blind or a selfish person like Akortorku would not see and acknowledge, Nanor concluded.

Chapter 7

Nene Tsatsu's marital life before he became chief was full of love and peace. He met Naki when both of them were students at Kankan Secondary School. But real courtship did not start until they had left school. That was when he was working at Akoso Industries. The long period between their first meeting and marriage gave them ample time to study and know each other very well. So they lived like a brother and a sister, each respecting the other's likes and dislikes; knowing that since they were from different families, there would be some differences in mannerisms.

Yes, they did occasionally disagree with each other since life is not always smooth, but whenever they exchanged harsh words, it was within their four walls. So nobody heard of them. Both of them understood that one's dirty clothes should not be washed in public. Nene Tsatsu used to tell friends that he did not marry Naki because she was pretty. They tied the knot because she was intelligent and extremely understanding.

Their happy and peaceful marriage life was, however, a surprise to most people. This was because of the resistance and the antagonism that characterized the marriage arrangement. Both families were strongly against their union because they were from different tribes and so they feared their marriage would not work. Members of Naki's family were more uncompromising in their determination not to allow the marriage to take place. Her father even warned her that any insistence on her part would mean a break in relations and that would result in disowning her.

This was not an isolated case. It was a common problem many young men and women who wanted to marry people of their choice always encountered in those days. It was the belief that marriages were more successful when the couples came from the same tribe and shared the same traditions and customs.

But Nene Tsatsu and Naki had a different opinion. They believed marriage had no barriers, and that its success depended largely on love and understanding and not on where one came from. So they went ahead visiting each other, and even staying together occasionally before the marriage actually took place, to the chagrin of their parents.

When the two families saw that they could not dissuade the couple from coming together, they turned against each other.

Each family blamed the other for not putting much pressure on them to break their relationship. This blame and counter-blame developed into a squabble, to the embarrassment of the couple, and most people in the village.

Nene Tsatsu and Naki did not want the prolonged opposition to their relationship to delay their marriage or derail it. So they reported the situation to the priest at the local church at Kesua. When the expatriate priest became convinced that they were actually in love with each other, he mobilized some of the church members and went to Adoma with them. There he had meetings with the parents of Nene Tsatsu and Naki. At these meetings, the parents were made to understand that a marriage, whether the couple were from the same tribe or not, could only be successful if the couple were actually in love. And from the interview he had with Nene Tsatsu and Naki, he could testify that they were really in love. So he appealed to the parents to allow them to get married.

It took a long time of education and persuasion before the two families finally threw-in the towel, and agreed to allow the marriage to go on. After the marriage, the couple enjoyed a wonderful life in the city where he was working before his coronation. Nene Tsatsu therefore hoped that the same happy life would continue at the village.

He was a source of human kindness to Naki, very concerned and excellently responsible. She on the other hand was full of love, intelligence and industry. But the main connection between them was the love and mutual understanding which bound them together. While they were in the city, they were a gem, a real example of a successful marriage, and people envied them. Their neighbors, and even casual visitors, always spoke well of them.

But soon after Nene Tsatsu's enthronement and his marriage to a traditional stool wife in addition to Naki, the peace and tranquility that was associated with their marriage started to wane. Abla, unlike Naki, was typically an illiterate village traditional woman. That notwithstanding, she was to behave in a manner befitting the wife of a chief. But that was on the contrary. No sooner had she moved into the palace than she started to show her true colors. She was envious, naggy and extremely quarrelsome. She would not accept the fact that Naki was the first wife and so she was senior to her. She was also unhappy with the arrangements Nene Tsatsu made in which she was asked to be responsible for traditional activities while Naki took charge of social and ceremonial matters. So always she complained and picked quarrels with Naki and even with their husband, at the least opportunity.

In order to prevent this unpleasant situation occurring all the times, Nene Tsatsu always made sure he was impartial in his dealings with his wives. He gave them equal attention and the same number of public engagements every week. This, of course, depended on the number of activities lined up for him. In spite of this, she always found cause to complain or quarrel with Naki, sometimes about trivial and ridiculous matters.

One day, Nene Tsatsu went to the city accompanied by Naki. At the headquarters of Christ Church, he had discussions with the Supervisor of Schools about the completed school block, and the role the church would like to play in its management. He also visited his former working place and discussed matters of mutual interest with his former employers and friends. He was happy with his visit to the city because both parties showed interest in his plans for the development of Adoma and promised assistance in various ways.

At about six o'clock in the evening, Nene Tsatsu returned to the palace. While he was in his bedroom changing from his European dress to a traditional one, Naki made her way to the dining hall to find out if Nene's dinner was ready. To her surprise there was no food on the table.

Then she went into the kitchen only to find out that no cooking had been done at all and Abla was nowhere to be found.

So Naki went to Nene Tsatsu in the chamber and said:

'Nene, you may stay in and rest while I cook something for you.'

'Cook something for me?' 'Is dinner not ready?'

'No, Nene. I went to check and no cooking had been done.'

'What? Is Abla not the one to cook for me today?'

Naki did not know what to say and so she quickly left him for the kitchen. Nene Tsatsu was confused. He wanted an explanation but he did not know whether to ask his attendant to go and look for Abla, or wait for her to come back home.

When tradition compelled him to marry Abla, in addition to Naki, care-taking arrangement was agreed upon by both wives. One of them was to take care and cook for him for three consecutive days then the other would take over for the same number of days. This arrangement was religiously adhered to by both wives and he never disappointed them or refused to take their meals. It was only on one occasion that he could not eat Abla's lunch. That was when he went to the city and was invited to lunch by some friends at the Star Hotel. On his return home, he explained to Abla why he could not eat again, and he thought she understood him. That was a long time ago.

Since then Nene Tsatsu had travelled out to the city or elsewhere but he always made sure he took his meals on his return home. He therefore saw no reason why Abla should not cook for him on this occasion. While he was trying to find out what prevented Abla from cooking for him, he was alarmed by a loud noise emanating from the direction of the kitchen. So he got up immediately and sat at the edge of the bed to ascertain what the noise was about. Soon he became convinced that his wives were quarrelling. He could hear the voice of Abla, and voices of other women trying to arrest the situation and restore sanity. Nene Tsatsu was terribly disturbed and even ashamed of what he was hearing. He did not want the commotion to continue and create a larger scene. So he decided to go out to intervene and restore order and sanity.

As he walked toward the kitchen, he could hear women appealing to both wives to stop the feud as a respect for the palace. They were about eight in number but Abla would not listen to them. The more they tried to take her away from the scene, the more she tried to disentangle herself from them and charge toward the kitchen. Naki could not stand Abla's insults either. So, occasionally, she would come out of the kitchen and hit back at her. The women, however, were not in favor of Naki's responses. They wanted her to be quiet because the more she retorted the more Abla became incensed and more uncontrollable.

Even when Nene Tsatsu appealed to her to be patient and go in with him so that he could listen to her grievances, she did not show any respect. This annoyed one of the women who, in her displeasure, rebuked her by saying;

'Oh! Abla, will you not listen even to Nene? What kind of behavior is this?'

'This is very disgraceful. You are disgracing yourself and the palace, Abla,' added another woman. It was at this stage that she calmed down and started showing signs of humility. This made everybody happy. But it was short-lived. Thinking that Abla had really calmed down, Nene Tsatsu asked his attendant to tell both wives to meet him in the palace to sort out the matter between them. When this message was relayed to Abla, she became furious again. She rushed to the chief, saying:

'I am not going to sit down for any talks because it will not make any difference.' Then she accused Nene Tsatsu of taking sides with Naki whenever there was a misunderstanding between them.

Nene Tsatsu denied the allegation against him but Abla insisted it was true and asked him whether he did not take Naki to the city most of the time. Then in an aggressive manner, she asked Nene to wait there and then she dashed into the palace. Everybody knew she was up to doing something despicable because she was muttering as she went away.

Just as the peace-makers suspected, Abla returned still talking to herself, and then she unblushingly threw something in front of Nene Tsatsu, saying: 'take your keys. You think I am a fool. How can I keep mere keys in my room when the boxes containing your precious possessions are kept in Naki's room?'

'You still do not understand, Abla,' responded Nene Tsatsu. 'The boxes are locked and you have the keys, and so literally you are the owner.' But Abla would not reason. Instead, she walked away from him and out of the palace. Embarrassed as he was, Nene Tsatsu did not utter a word anymore. Rather, he was sorry for her because of her misunderstanding. The few people still around did not say anything because they did not understand what was going on and nobody was bold to ask. They were all confused. They looked on for a while and then dispersed.

The attendant picked the bunch of keys from the ground, and gave it to Nene Tsatsu. He looked at the bunch for a few seconds, signed, and then asked rhetorically, 'If someone is keeping locked boxes and you are keeping the keys to them, who is the actual owner of the things in the boxes?' Then he thanked the few people now left on the scene and went into the palace. Even though he was terribly shaken, he still felt sorry for Abla.

The bedroom that Naki was occupying was larger and so he kept most of his personal and traditional possessions there. When Abla moved into the palace, only a few of the boxes were moved into her care because her room was smaller and the chief did not want it to be congested. But with the knowledge of both wives, he kept the bunch of keys to all the boxes containing traditional materials in Abla's room which meant that Naki could not get anything from any of the boxes there without Abla's knowledge and consent. Literally, therefore, this decision gave her an authority over his possessions in the boxes.

That night Nene Tsatsu's mind was so filled with thoughts of what had happened during the day that he could not sleep. First he thought of Akortorku's clandestine activities aimed at undermining his rule. This occupied his mind for a while and then his thoughts shifted to his wife's disgraceful behavior. He considered their behavior more damaging to him than anything else because it affected his personal reputation and that of the palace. In his thoughts, he revisited all the scenarios leading to his coronation as chief of Adoma.

He starting with the death of the former chief and his nomination as a successor; he thought of how he stayed away from his own home while the royal delegation members were hunting him in the city; his dramatic encounter with the last delegation which ended up in his being taken to the village to be crowned. Then he thought of his marriage to Abla in the name of tradition, which he initially objected to. He did not regret consenting to be made a chief anyway. After all, it was a call to serve his people and village. What disturbed him though throughout the night was the behavior of his wives. He still felt he would have been happier as a chief if a stool wife had not come into his life.

Early the next day, Linguist Nanor and four other members of the council of elders visited Nene Tsatsu. They had heard of the deplorable fracas of the previous day and had come to tell him how disappointed they were, and to offer him support. There was unanimous condemnation of his wife's disgraceful behavior.

So a decision was taken to summon Naki and Abla to a Council meeting so that whatever grudge they had against each other could be looked into and the matter settled. It was also agreed that two relatives of each of the wives should be invited to this very important meeting which was scheduled for the evening.

Nene Tsatsu thanked his elders for their concern and wish for peace in the palace. However, he blamed the elders and the kingmakers for not telling him much about Abla and for rushing the marriage, which did not give him enough time to personally study her. He reminded them that all that they told him was "she was from a respectable family", forgetting that there could be a very good stock but its offspring could be despicable.

'This reminds me of the caution a very great dramatist, William Shakespeare, gave his audience in his play, Macbeth, more than four hundred years ago.' He told them:

'You cannot find the mind's construction in the face.' This is just like saying you cannot say a person comes from a good family and so she too will be of good character. He went on:

'Before Naki and I got married, we dated each other for years.

During these years, I turned her inside out, viewed all the instincts in her and saw that they were good. I became sure that we were compatible. Then in addition to the love we already have, we decided to get married. You see,' Nene Tsatsu continued, 'both love and compatibility are essential in marriage. They complement each other for a peaceful and lasting union between man and woman. I know a man who met a woman one day, both decided to get married the next month, and then a week later there was a divorce. This means either love or compatibility, or both, were lacking. There may be love but if there is no compatibility, the marriage may not last,' he ended.

The elders agreed with the chief and apologized to him for the rush during his marriage to Abla. They assured him that as a result of what he had pointed out to them, they would meet with all the kingmakers to discuss the tradition of a stool wife and find out what amendments could be made to that ancient practice. Then the meeting ended so that members could return to the palace early for the

85

settlement of the case between Naki and Abla, scheduled for the evening.

When the arbitration time came, Linguist Nanor acknowledged the presence of everyone and told them their presence, especially, the presence of the relatives of the wives, showed that all of them recognized the gravity of the problem. After Nene Tsatsu had put the case before the Council of elders, the wives were asked to say their version of the confrontation between them. It was found out that there were vast differences in their statements but there was no third person at the time the quarrel started to testify on each other's behalf. However, after examining the whole situation and taking everything into consideration, the council found Abla guilty.

She was made to understand that she failed in her responsibility to cook for her husband, and whatever the cause of her inability to do so was; she should not have done anything to provoke Naki's anger. The Council also found her behavior not worthy of a chief's wife. But she was not fined. Nene Tsatsu produced two bottles schnapps which were used to settle the case and bring peace between the wives.

Then they were strongly admonished to be of good behavior all the times. As wives of the chief, they were reminded that all eyes were on them and so their light had to shine brightly in peace to uphold the dignity of the chieftaincy. Everybody, including the relatives of the wives, was happy with the settlement and so the case was put to rest.

Chapter 8

In spite of Akortorku's treachery and the recent events at the palace, Nene Tsatsu continued to discharge his duties and execute his programs as planned. With the support of the people, the six-classroom school block was completed on time. And as expected, many people were present at its opening and dedication ceremony. The local people were there not only to admire their new school block, a citadel of knowledge and civilization, but also to see the visitors from the city.

Conspicuously absent were Akortorku and his few supporters. But that did not make any difference to Nene Tsatsu. In as much as he was not physically obstructing and preventing him from performing his duties to the people, he would not be bothered by his divisive actions. The invited guests included officials from the Ministry of Education and Christ Church Educational Unit. The two institutions responded favorably to Nene Tsatsu's request. Christ Church accepted to take over the management and administration of the school; but the overall supervision and payment of teachers' salaries were to be borne by the local Ministry of Education. The brief dedication was followed by many speeches and tributes paid to Nene Tsatsu and the people of Adoma.

The Inspector of Christ Church Schools was particularly happy about the completion of the school block, and thanked the people of Adoma for their foresight. He hoped they would work in the same spirit to complete the rehabilitation of the road, which they had already started. According to him, the road would bring Adoma closer to the city and the outside world, and ease problems for many people who would be visiting the town and school. In his closing speech, Nene Tsatsu thanked the people of Adoma for the spirit of cooperation they exhibited in putting up the school block, and the invited quests for their support and assistance. He hoped they would continue to work together in the same communal spirit for many years.

On the eve of the next working day, linguist Nanor and Akutey went to see Nene Tsatsu. The chief had already retired to bed but they insisted on seeing him. The attendant was therefore compelled to go in and inform him of the presence of his councilors. He came out very agitated because he had never been woken up from bed like that before. 'Is anything wrong?' He enquired.

'No, Nene. But something is about to happen,' Nanor replied. His voice was shaky which was unusual of him. One could detect immediately that he was apprehensive of imminent trouble.

'What is going to happen?' Nene Tsatsu asked while sitting down. 'Akortorku is going to give us a problem tomorrow.

He has told people and sworn that he will not allow the diversion of the road through his cocoa farm,' Nanor revealed.

'What? That is the only route which will not pose a serious problem to us, and he knows it. All of us agreed on this at our last meeting, isn't it?'

'Yes, Nene,' Akutey interjected and then continued: 'this means cutting down a few cocoa trees to make way for the road but Akortorku says anybody who does so will see blood.'

'We know Akortorku, Nene. He can do anything imaginable without looking back. That is why we are here,' said Nanor.

Nene Tsatsu was silent for some time. The two councilors were also quiet, obviously trying to think of what to do. When the chief broke the silence, he thanked his informants for letting him know of Akortorku's intentions. Then he insisted that the diversion must go on because the rehabilitation of the road would help in Adoma's development and transformation. He cited examples of many people in biblical and modern times who sacrificed even their lives so that others might benefit.

Therefore he did not think sacrificing a few cocoa trees so that a road could be constructed for the benefit of the people was too much to endure. He assured his elders that he would personally be present at the site the next day. Then he asked them to tell the people not to be fearful of Akortorku's threats. Early the next morning, Nene Tsatsu went to the Kesua police and reported his threats to them and then asked for protection at the site. He did not want to take chances.

When Nene Tsatsu arrived at the construction site, he was amazed to see an unusually large number of people already there. Apart from the able-bodied men who have all the times been involved in the community work, older men and women and even children were also there. The men were there with their implements but none of them had started work. A man approached Nene Tsatsu and suggested that work should not start until the arrival of Akortorku. But Nene objected to the suggestion and gave an order for work to start. This was received with mixed reactions and murmurings from a section of the people. But Nene Tsatsu ignored them. He knew nobody wanted to be the first to start work and so he decided to lead the way. Then the other workers followed.

They had a few meters of clearing to do before the detour so work proceeded without fear and interruption. Trees were hewed, stumps and rocks were excavated and the created holes filled-in. Then the surface of the road was smoothened. Within a short time, work was completed up to the point where the diversion would take place. Nene Tsatsu and some of the brave men surveyed the route again to the other side of the hill where the detour would rejoin the main road. This was done to prevent any unnecessary felling of trees or any other commercial trees. All this time nothing happened but it could be seen that many of the people there were apprehensive of Akortorku's threats.

Nene Tsatsu and the other surveyors returned to the detour point and gave the all clear for work to proceed. He personally moved forward, a saw in his hand, and as soon as he raised it up to strike, Akortorku surfaced out of the blue with a short gun in his hand. He stood at a distance and roared:

'Anybody who destroys my cocoa trees will be joining his ancestors immediately, and I mean it. The trees are dear to me because they are the source of my family's livelihood.'

Everybody was stunned and filled with fear. They were too afraid to say anything. Nene Tsatsu looked straight into his face and said:

'I hope you don't mean what you want to do, Akortorku. You were at our Council meeting when all of us agreed that in order to rehabilitate the road, we have to divert it eastward,' he reminded him.

'Yes, I was present but I was not in favor of the diversion. The cocoa trees are my life,' he replied.

'Our decision remains unchanged, Akortorku,' Nene Tsatsu made it clear to him. Then he added like a preacher, 'In this world, one has to sacrifice one thing or another, in one way or the other, for others to benefit. Our ancestors you just talked about sacrificed many things, some even sacrificed their own lives so that others could live in peace. Therefore Akortorku, please, allow work to continue. 'If you want to be compensated, let us know and we shall do so.' Nene Tsatsu concluded. His offer was followed by several appeals from the concerned workers. Even people returning from the market stopped and appealed to him to stop his opposition. When these market people saw the gun in his hands, they could not help wailing, as if somebody had already been shot. But Akortorku was not moved by their cries. Instead, he reiterated his stance that he did not want his cocoa trees to be destroyed. But Nene Tsatsu was undaunted and uncompromising.

There was no way the diversion of the road could take place without cutting or uprooting all trees in its way. So he fearlessly reiterated that, in the name of the people of Adoma and their ancestors and in the name of God Almighty, the work had to be done. The whole place became very quiet as tension heightened. Nene Tsatsu looked at him in the face and surveyed the area around him and then gave the order for work to proceed. He personally moved forward and started sawing a branch of a cocoa tree. This inflamed Akortorku's anger and aimed his gun at the chief. The cowards among the people beat a hasty retreat in fear. But he could not pull the trigger. Rather he roared:

'I will kill you, I will kill you all.'

Meanwhile, other brave men joined Nene Tsatsu and Nanor in the work, felling trees in their way as they moved forward. But Akortorku could not pull the trigger. However, his gun was still pointing at the chief. At this time, he was perspiring profusely, and shaking. Apart from a few women who were still begging and appealing to him to allow the work to go on, everybody else was quiet. For once, he shifted his attention to a section of the crowd and then gradually and shamefully, he lowered the gun without uttering a word. Just as he was about to walk away, the Kesua police arrived and took him away. Everybody was relieved and wondered how the police got to know about what Akortorku had planned to do.

The construction of the road continued without any more opposition. And surprisingly, the number of people that turned up for work increased every working day.

Remarkably, even women came to participate in the work. Some of them brought food and water to the workers because they knew the road, when completed, would bring salvation to them. They would no more be carrying heavy loads of foodstuffs on their heads to Kesua market.

In strict adherence to the advice Jesus Christ gave mankind in the Bible that we should: 'Ask and we shall be given, seek and we shall find,' Nene Tsatsu approached the District Department of Transport, the local Private Road Transport Owners Association and some road contractors in the city, and appealed to them for their assistance to enable them complete the road. The response he received was amazing. Almost all the people he had discussions with praised the people of Adoma for embarking on developmental projects in their village instead of waiting for government to do everything for them.

At the end, Nene Tsatsu left the city a happy man because most of the people he had meetings with pledged to play a role in the construction of the road. Soon afterward, technical and material assistance, including heavy machinery to deal with the rocky sections of the road, started arriving on site. This accelerated and made the work easier for the workers. The news of Akortorku's shooting attempt on Nene Tsatsu spread to all corners of Adoma, and soon, he became a subject of discussions both at work and at home. Many people condemned what he had tried to do and branded him 'an enemy of the people'. It was learnt, later on, that the police did not charge him. Instead, he was asked to sign an undertaking to be of good behavior and to cooperate with Nene Tsatsu in the work he was doing to develop Adoma.

Nene Tsatsu combined overseeing the road work with his normal traditional duties. He wanted the road to be completed before the scheduled funeral rites of the late chief because he knew visitors would be converging on Adoma during the ceremony. He was concerned mainly with people in Kesua and the city who might like to come to the funeral. These people would certainly travel in cars or on buses and if the road was not completed, it would be impossible for them to attend the funeral. So he wanted to road to be completed without any unnecessary delay.

Already, the funeral rites had taken too long to be performed as a result of the fact that it took the elders a long time to have a new chief installed. Therefore Nene Tsatsu felt a postponement or a further delay to perform the funeral rites would make the spirit of the late chief more restless and unhappy. This made him remember a similar situation he was told about. A chief died and because of disagreements between the royal families, his successor could not be agreed upon. That delayed the crowning of a new chief and the funeral rites of the late chief for years. His spirit became very restless and unhappy and so it started haunting the elders and the kingmakers. The kingmakers realized that his ghost was haunting them because of their failure to perform his final funeral rites to make him rest in peace. So a compromise was quickly reached with the royal families, and a new chief was installed immediately. As soon as the funeral rites were performed for the late chief, his ghost stopped appearing to the kingmakers.

Nene Tsatsu did not want them to be in the same situation and so he prayed that nothing should happen to delay the completion of the road so that the late chief's final rites could be held as planned. His prayers were therefore answered when after eighteen months, the road was completed; thanks to the Almighty God and the technical and material support obtained from institutions and people outside Adoma.

Officials from the District Office and members of the Kesua Drivers Union were present at the opening ceremony. In his speech, the District Chief Executive applauded the people and told them they had done what all governments all over the world wanted people to do; that was, to try to embark on projects that would help improve their quality of life. He made them understand that government could not do everything for every city, town and village, and so it was vital for people of every neighborhood to come together to do the things they could that would help develop their areas. He, however, reminded them that "God helps those who help themselves" and so government was always prepared to assist those who engage in developmental projects.

After the Chief Executive's speech, one of the invited traditional chiefs and the president of the Private Drivers Union also spoke. All of them praised the people of Adoma for their foresight and community spirit that had helped them to rehabilitate the road. At the end of the speeches, an announcement was made that one of the drivers had offered to take the first set of passengers to Kesua free of charge. This driver was popularly known as "Lucky Day". There was an inscription, "FORGET THE PAST", written boldly both at the front and back of his lorry. As soon as the announcement was made, people started scrambling for seats. It was the survival of the fittest which many people were displeased about. Soon the truck was full but Nene

Tsatsu was not happy with the disorderly way people were struggling to get seats on the truck. So he asked Nanor to see that as many women as possible got seats and the opportunity to have the free ride. All the men were therefore asked to disembark to give their seats to the women, otherwise the lorry would not move.

While the men were alighting, some people spotted Akortorku. How he got on board nobody had any idea. When he was released by the police, he went to the palace and expressed his sorrow and apology to Nene Tsatsu. But everybody knew it was not from his heart because he did not take part in the construction of the road.

Therefore many people were astounded, not only to see him at the official opening of the road but also to be one of the first to board the lorry. One of the men who first recognized him cried out: 'That is Akortorku, I will not forget the past,' in apparent reference to what was written on the lorry.

Those who really knew what he was actually referring to laughed sarcastically.

While Nanor was directing the women to board the lorry, Akortorku, together with some of the men who first charged onto the truck left the scene as the people scoffed derisively. Soon they became swallowed by the crowd. When Nene Tsatsu was informed about Akortorku's presence, he asked the people to allow him to be judged by his own conscience. He told them it was not necessary to think of incidents of the past anymore and added that what was worth thinking about, were events to come, especially the final funeral rites of the late, Nene Tsatsu.

On the next market day only a few people carried foodstuffs to Kesua. There were three vehicles at Adoma to convey people and their foodstuffs to the market. Everybody felt relieved of the tension and nightmare that had characterized market days in the past.

Chapter 9

The final funeral rites of the previous chief came on as scheduled. Nene Tsatsu 11 was a great chief. It was he who led the Kabos down the hills during the koro wars and brought them down to their new home at the plains. It was also he who first started the construction of the road from Kesua to Adoma, and so many people loved him. As a result of his popularity, a great number of people, including well-wishers from the city and neighboring villages attended the funeral rites.

As people moved about on that day, one could see only the color red or black. These were the colors of the funeral cloth that was used for the occasion. Around the people's heads or wrists were tied bands of the red or black cloths matching the color of the funeral dress. On an occasion like this, the Asafo companies and the musical groups could not be left out. So they were in attendance in their numbers. The most dominant ones were the Obonu and the Oglodjo groups which were associated with the court more than others. The musical instruments were also decorated with red or black ribbons or bands to be in line with the cloths the people had on.

Since the occasion was the final funeral rites of a late chief, the Obonu music featured more prominently. The instruments of this palace music consisted of a pair of drums made of wood, about four feet high, and another shorter pair. These shorter ones were the female drums. Each end was tightly covered with a sheepskin. This is where the beating took place. The male and female drums were accompanied by another instrument, the 'gong-gong.' which provided a melodious accompaniment. All the instruments were draped with the funeral red or black cloths.

The Obonu music and dance started on Thursday, the day the funeral rites officially started. Members of the group were mainly grown-up men and women. This composition contrasted sharply with the younger members of the Oglodjo group whose members were made up of younger men and women. Early in the morning, members of the group assembled at the chief's palace and started performing. On this day, the rites involved only Nene Tsatsu and his elders and kingmakers, the family members of the late chief, and invited chiefs and royal people. When it was time for the ritual to start, the drummers were asked to stop. Then libation was poured in honor of the late chief, followed by dirges, sung by the women. In the evening, the people left the palace for the royal mausoleum. The drummers and all the women stayed at the palace because the rituals there involved only men. As usual, libation was poured, and then various rituals were performed, followed by the singing of dirges. This lasted late into the night.

Friday was the highlight of the funeral rites. As early as seven o'clock in the morning, most houses in Adoma, the chief's family house, the palace and the entire village were already crowded. And at the time the ceremony actually started the village was bursting. At Laasi ground where the main ceremony took place, one could hardly hear anything because of the deafening music.

Both Obonu and Oglojo groups were in action, as well as the all-women Ahusabe musical ensemble. In each group, the music and dancing went on like mad, as if each group was trying to out-do the other. The Ahusabe and Oglojo dancers danced more gracefully unlike the Obonu dancers who danced aggressively. Many people were apparently happy and excited to see them dance. Their dance always attracted large crowds.

There was quiet only when all the chiefs and the invited guests took their seats. After the usual pouring of libation to ask for blessings from the Almighty God and the ancestors, other rites were performed in honor of the late chief. These were followed by a tribute from Chief Nene Tsatsu 111, and then other speeches or tributes by some of the invited chiefs and dignitaries followed.

The actual celebration of the late chief's life started after the speeches when the musical groups took over activities. People could not help dancing to their favorite music. The chiefs danced too, mostly to the Obonu music. They danced in honor of their late brother with their swords in their hands. The chief whose dancing was most spectacular and attracted a tremendous attention and admiration was Chief Koley of Tapon.

When he got up, he lowered his cover-cloth down to his waist. Then he moved to the center of the Obonu group. There, he faced the east and pointed his sword to that direction. He turned to face the west and pointed the sword to that direction too. Then he started dancing, slowly and slowly; and then in quick steps, simultaneously moving his sword up and down, as if he was cutting something in his way. Occasionally, he would hop on one foot and swing the other round in a whirlwind fashion. While he was dancing, his women admirers sang praise songs punctuating them with the appellation: 'amio o ami.' (Man born on Saturday.) At the end of the dancing, chief Koley pointed his sword to the east again and bowed.

While the drumming and dancing was going on, the mobile warriors and members of the Asafo companies went up and down and in and out of the surrounding houses singing war songs and dirges attributed to the late chief. They wore only raffia skirts and their bodies and faces were besmeared with a red substance. This made them look very scary and frightful. When they got to the chief's palace, they opened the doors and looked into them as if they were looking for the late chief. After going round for some time, they returned to the ceremonial ground, planted themselves behind the Obonu musicians and joined in the music. Once a while, some of them fired their guns into the air while others danced in an acrobatic way.

As the evening drew nearer, the singing of dirges and the firing of guns heightened. Food and drinks were provided and it was evident that the men got extra energy from the local gin they took. So the tumult continued, reaching fever-heat. The drums beat violently, and the men and women leapt up and down in frenzy. They were all filled with the spirit of the dance. As the guns continued to be fired, sparks flew out repeatedly and filled the atmosphere with dust and smoke. The tall coconut and palmnut trees were the victims. Their fronds and branches fell one after another as the guns were fired toward them.

Suddenly, there was a cry of agony and horror where the Obonu musicians were performing. The world quickly stood still and everything stopped immediately. In the middle of the Obonu dancers lay Asawatse Kwam, a noble man from the Sasu family. A gun Detse was using accidentally exploded, and a piece of iron from it hit him while he was dancing. It was a terrifying sight. People rushed to his aid and seeing the gravity of his condition, he was rushed to the hospital at Kesua. But unfortunately, he did not make it. He died before they got to there.

The news of Asawatse Kwam's death was received by the people with great shock. Every activity at the ceremonious ground ceased immediately, and people expressed their emotions frantically in various ways. There were wailings and sweeping, and even questions, asking the gods and the ancestors why such a death should occur at that time. Tragic deaths had happened in Adoma before but they were not caused by a fellow Adomaian. This was the reason why some of the people, especially those from Kwam's family, were very furious. But there was another reason why they should be angry.

Traditionally in Adoma, people believed that an unnatural death was the result of a curse by the gods. So anybody who died in an accident, like Asawatse Kwam, was not accorded the normal burial rites. That was because his death was considered an abomination. And so according to tradition, his body was not even laid in state. Every rite had to be performed at the scene of the death by fetish priests, and the body committed for burial after special customary rites. These rites were to cleanse the family and the scene of the accident; and appeal to the gods not to allow such deaths to happen again.

If, however, the family members wanted to lay the body in state to honor it in some way, a special shed had to be erected outside the house for this purpose. Even in this case, the fetish priests had to perform all the necessary rites, including the burial, and not the family members. This is one of the reasons why the family members of Asawatse Kwam were naturally angry. They felt the family had been put to shame.

Nene Tsatsu hurriedly held an emergency meeting with the councilors concerning his death. All members expressed their shock and sorrow to hear of his death. However, it was agreed that the celebration of the late chief's life should continue, and the court messenger was asked to convey that decision to the people. Since the accident resulted in death, two members were sent to Kesua to report it to the police on behalf of Nene Tsatsu 111. Another two elders were asked to go to the family of the late Kwam to express the palace's heartfelt sorrow and condolences to his wife and relatives.

The police came to the village to see Nene Tsatsu 111 the following day, and Detse was taken to the police station for questioning. Later, Nene Tsatsu also went to the police station to give a formal statement, as requested by the police. At the end of his statement, he asked for the withdrawal of the case to be settled out of the criminal court, in the light of the circumstances leading to the death of the late Kwam. The chief's request for a bail was granted. But he was told that the docket would not be closed until a peaceful settlement had been made, agreeable to all sides. So he was asked to let the police know as soon as this was done.

At the end of the late chief's final funeral rites, Nene Tsatsu 111 invited Detse and the relatives of the late Kwam for talks. He hoped that such a meeting would provide the platform to all sides to air their views or grievances and find out how to solve the case peacefully. But the late Kwam's family members refused to attend this meeting. Instead, they had a family meeting at which they expressed their anger at the death of their beloved Kwam and the withdrawal of the case from the police.

They wanted Detse to be tried at the criminal court instead of the Tradition Council where they did not expect the outcome to be what they wanted. So they decided to revenge on Detse and Nene Tsatsu for bailing him and withdrawing the case from the police. Nobody knew how Akortorku got to know about the decision that the late Kwam's family had taken because he was not a member of that family. But soon, he became a party to the plan to retaliate on Detse and Nene Tsatsu.

Since the diversion of the road incident and its official opening, he had been looking for an opportunity to personally confront Nene Tsatsu. The unfortunate death of the late Kwam gave him that chance. So he had several meetings with late Kwam's family members and supported all decisions taken against Detse and Nene Tsatsu 111.

He was instrumental in the decision to withdraw the recognition of Nene as Chief of Adoma. When a committee was formed to select someone to succeed the late Kwam as leader of the Sasu family, he forced himself into it even though he was not a family member.

Nene Tsatsu did not know about Akortorku's clandestine activities to undermine and destroy him until he was confronted on his way to the city by the Sasu people as he passed through their zone. While some of them hooted at him, others hurled stones at his car and insulted him. After experiencing this hostility for the second time, he asked his linguist to investigate. It was after Nanor's investigation that he got to know that Akortorku had joined the family of the late Kwam to wage war on him.

When a new leader was appointed to succeed the late Kwam, he sent a congratulatory message to the family but it was not warmly received and neither was it acknowledged. Again, during the presentation ceremony of Asawatse Kodjo, the new leader of the Sasu people, Nene Tsatsu sent a delegation to the ceremony but it was not given the necessary royal recognition. It was at this time that he realized that the Sasu people and Akortorku were at total war with him and that they really wanted to destroy him. To him that was unfortunate. He did not want the death of late Kwam, painful as it was, to divide Adoma and damage the unity and development that was evolving in the village.

So he convened another meeting this time of all clan leaders and members of the council of elders. Detse was also invited to this meeting. But when the time came, Nene Tsatsu was painfully disappointed. The key players in the case he wanted to settle, Asawatse Kodjo, who succeeded the late Kwam and Akortorku and Goku from the other royal family, blatantly refused to attend the meeting. Therefore the main item on the agenda; the accident that led to Kwam's death and the animosity that resulted, could not be discussed in detail. So after discussing other related matters, the meeting came to an end.

While Nene Tsatsu was still thinking of how to bring all the parties to come together for a peaceful settlement of the rift, his opponents had their own meeting. Naturally everybody regretted the death of Kwam and was sorry about it. But nobody was happy with the role Akortorku was playing. That was because he had hijacked the situation and taken it as an opportunity to oppose and make life uncomfortable to the chief. Present at this meeting were Asawatse Kodjo and the elders from the Sasu family and members of the other royal family led by Akortorku and Goku. The Sasu people were aggrieved because the way their former leader died made his death ignominious. They were also unhappy that Nene Tsatsu did not allow the case to be heard by the civil court.

Akortorku, on the other hand, had a different agenda. He was unhappy with the change of the rule governing the succession to the seat of the chief under which Nene Tsatsu became the chief of Adoma. In addition to that, he felt Nene Tsatsu was too young and immature. He often told people age was experience and experience was a very important asset in traditional governance. So he was able to sway people to his side by drumming his feelings and ideas into them and using their support in his villainous activities against the chief. The diversion of the road through his cocoa farm which he was unhappy about gave him more ammunition to use to undermine the chief.

At the meeting, the two parties agreed to continue to shun all activities of the chief until their grievances were addressed. The happiest person was Akortorku who failed on two occasions in his confrontation with the chief to disorganize him. He hoped that the alliance that they had formed and their agreement to shun Nene Tsatsu would help him to achieve his personal avowed objectives. So it could be seen that while the family members of the late Kwam had genuine reason to be aggrieved, Akortorku and his people were just utilizing the situation to their own selfish aim. As a member of the Traditional Council, he was supposed to be present at meetings and be part of the decision-making machinery. On the contrary, he displayed his irresponsibility and unpatriotic tendencies by refusing to attend Council meetings, and continued to wage war on the chief.

Chapter 10

In spite of Akortorku's absence at meetings and his wicked actions to undermine him, Nene Tsatsu 111 was not perturbed. He carried on with his normal duties at the palace and in the community, unruffled. One Sunday when people saw him going to worship at the newly established People's Church, no eye-brows were raised. They considered his action a wise move since he was the chief and father of the people. But when his fellowship with members of People's Church became very regular, people became concerned and began to ask questions. They did not understand why he should break faith with Christ Church and shift his allegiance to the other church. He had been a devoted member of Christ Church ever since his childhood. His parents were among the first to embrace it when it was first brought to the village by the white missionaries, and they were still staunch members.

Soon rumors became rife, each giving reasons why Nene Tsatsu converted into the People's Church faith. This heightened the anxiety of many people who were eager to know what actually made their chief stop attending church services at Christ Church. Within a short time, one of the rumors became more credible. It gave a full account of the events that compelled him to switch to the People's Church. The rumor became authentic when it was corroborated by some members of the royal household. They stated that the chief was compelled to go to the People's Charismatic Church because of an incident that took place during the hearing of a case at the palace.

This case started late afternoon and lasted into the night. Earlier on, two other cases were settled peacefully and without any incident. The complainant, Padi, alleged that he bought a piece of land from Terku, and then the respondent resold that same land to another person. He did not know about it until he started cultivating it when he was challenged by the third person. Both the complainant and the respondent were given time to tell the traditional court their versions of the case. After questions were put to both of them, witnesses were called to testify. The last person to be called was Atter, the second person who also claimed ownership of the land. But from what he said and the statements of other witnesses, it was evident that he bought the land months after it was sold to Terku. After all the witnesses had been heard, the councilors retired to consult with each other before giving verdict.

When they returned, Linquist Nanor announced that the court had found Padi guilty of selling the land to Atter when he had already sold it to Terku. Then Nanor told them that Nene Tsatsu would explain their decision further to them. But after uttering only three words, Nene Tsatsu stopped suddenly, screamed and then cried out loudly:

'Get away from me. I don't want you here. Get away, I say.'

As he screamed, he covered his face with his left hand and was behaving abnormally. The elders were filled with surprise and terror because they did not know who he was talking to. Nanor rushed to him, and while trying to console him, asked him who he was speaking to. When he became calm and normal again, Nene Tsatsu told his people that he saw an image in the exact form of the late Kwam staring at him and blinding him. Then in apologizing for the interruption of proceedings, he assured the people that there was nothing wrong with him physically and mentally. The councilors however ruled out any possibility of the late Kwam's ghost haunting him since he was not the direct cause of his death.

But they were mistaken. Kwam's spirit was unhappy that Nene Tsatsu used his influence to prevent his killer from appearing before a criminal court. So he came to revenge his death not on Detse but on the chief. When he began to talk again, the ghost appeared. Like on the first occasion, nobody else saw it apart from Nene Tsatsu. He screamed again frantically, got up from his seat and started to move backward, forgetting that the wall was right behind him. Almost all the councilors rushed to his aid. He was shaking and perspiring profusely as they helped him back to his seat.

A decision was hurriedly taken to stop business. After all, the verdict of the case under discussion had already been decided and agreed. This was to give Nene Tsatsu time to rest. Throughout the evening, nothing happened. He took his dinner normally and played with his children until it was time to go to bed. Normally, he did not like sleeping when lights were on, but this time Abla suggested that he should leave the light on since it was believed that ghosts did not appear under bright lights. But when he retired to bed, he could not sleep. The thought of his uninvited guest did not make him fall asleep early. When eventually he fell asleep, the ghost appeared again, just like in a dream and again he screamed loudly, telling it to stop terrorizing him. Then it immediately vanished. Naki, whose bedroom was next to his came out and ran to him.

As soon as she entered his room, Nene Tsatsu started reprimanding her for not filling the lantern with enough oil. This was because the lantern was off and he thought it was empty since the wick was not burning. Naki was shocked. She took the lantern and shook it to find out if really there was no oil in it. But it was not. The oil in it could last for another day or two. Both of them then concluded that the light was probably put off by the ghost.

The appearance of the spirit continued for three nights and during these nights, Nene Tsatsu could not have a sound sleep. The spirit manifested in many different forms; in normal ordinary form, in the way he was dressed when he was dancing, and at the time he was struggling on the ground after he had been hit by the stray metal. Sometimes he would not see the spirit but he could hear his last words: 'Oh, you have killed me.' And these echoed in his hears repeatedly. On the fourth day, a report was made to the priest of Christ Church. It was unwise now to consider his terrifying condition a private matter.

When the priest visited Nene Tsatsu and was briefed on what was happening to the chief, he ruled out the possibility of Kwam's ghost haunting him. He attributed his experiences to sheer imagination, adding that what he claimed he was seeing were, in fact, hallucinations.

'There is nothing like a spirit roaming the earth or haunting a person,' he stressed and went on; 'When one dies, it is only his body that dies and remains on earth. His spirit leaves him and goes back to our Father in heaven,' he concluded.

'But I saw the spirit several times in the exact form of the late Kwam, and what I heard him say was exactly what he said when he was lying on the ground,' Nene Tsatsu argued.

Even though the priest was not convinced by what he was told, he asked the chief and his wives to join him in prayers. He prayed for the chief for about thirty minutes asking God to deliver him from whatever was happening to him. At the end of the prayers, he invited the chief to the church where more prayers were said for him during the evening prayer session.

But the prayers did not prevent the ghost from appearing to Nene Tsatsu. That night it appeared twice and both wives had difficult times soothing and comforting their husband. As a result of this disturbing situation, all his duties were temporally suspended. Official traditional functions were vested in the hands of the elder kingmaker and Linguist Nanor. Nene Tsatsu was strictly kept indoors and the public was informed that he was indisposed. This was to prevent any embarrassment in case the evil spirit appeared to him in public. But many people, however, got to know of his problem and reacted in various ways. A majority was sympathetic of and felt sorry for him.

As soon as Akortorku heard of Nene Tsatsu's strange situation, he hurriedly called for a meeting of his supporters, and proposed a motion for his removal from office. He told them the chief's strange behavior was nothing short of insanity and the people of Adoma could not risk having a mad chief. That would be a curse to the stool, he told them. This was agreed by all the conspirators, but they felt they could not execute the motion without seeking the mandate of the general public. They had to be sure a majority of the people agreed with them. So they decided to give themselves time to rally more people behind them. Another meeting was therefore scheduled for that purpose.

As Nene Tsatsu's incomprehensive problem spread all over Adoma, some members of the People's Charismatic Church heard about it and felt their pastor would be able to drive the spirit away from him. Two of the members therefore went to the palace to find out if the elder kingmaker and Linguist Nanor, who were deputizing for the chief, would agree to transfer him to the People's Charismatic Church for healing. They were told the senior pastor, popularly known as Prophet Yohana, had power to counteract the activities of evil spirits that roamed the earth, and drive them away from people tormented by them. In order to convince them, the church members gave them several examples of victims Prophet Yohana had delivered from situations like the one Nene Tsatsu was going through.

This information was given to the chief and even though for many years he had been a staunch member of Christ Church, he agreed to be taken to the People's Charismatic Church for his healing. Arrangements were made and Nene Tsatsu was taken to the church one morning. There Prophet

113

Yohana told them the devil was not more powerful than the Almighty God and that the chief would be free within two days. Then with the aid of his assistants, a long and powerful prayer was said for the chief as incenses were burnt and Florida water was sprinkled on him. At the end of the prayers, Prophet Yohana asked them to go back home and get ready for more prayers which would be said in the palace in the evening.

Prophet Yohana arrived at the palace for the second session of prayers dressed in his official white robes, holding a bible. He was accompanied by two assistants, one also holding a bible and incense, and the other, a bottle of holy water. First the incense was lighted and given to the Prophet and then he asked to be led to the chief's bedroom. There he said a short prayer, praising God and asking the Holy Spirit to take control of the entire palace and make the devil powerless. When he returned, he asked the chief to be seated in the middle of the living room, and made his wives and the elders stand by him. He sprinkled the holy water on them and with the burning incense in his hand; he went round Nene Tsatsu and his people three times. Then the actual prayers to deliver the chief from the evil spirit started.

It was in English but occasionally, it would change into unfamiliar words and the chief and his people would be at a loss. After praying for about thirty minutes, the Prophet stretched his right hand and placed it on the head of the chief while reciting some mystical words. Then he intensified the prayers, condemning the devil in the name of our Lord Jesus Christ and asking God to drive the spirit away from Nene Tsatsu just as He chased Satan from Heaven. Soon darkness started to fill the hall and the presence of God was felt. Once a while, the people could see some shining objects like stars hovering around them, making it look as if Heaven had come down to earth.

At this stage, Prophet Yohana broke the prayers and asked Nene Tsatsu and his people to kneel down. Then he intensified the prayers again, this time in a language foreign to them. A strong wind blew through the hall and then through the entire palace as the prayers went on. When the winds stopped, the stars hovering around them became brighter and then simultaneously vanished. Prophet Yohana then ended the prayers and exclaimed:

'Praise the Lord. It is done, it is done, Alleluia. The evil spirit is not more powerful than the Almighty God who created all things. Lord, we thank you for listening to us.' Then he asked the people to join him in singing the song:

'Alleluia, Alleluia, Alleluia.

The strife is over, the battle is done.

Now is the victors' triumph won,

O let the song of praise be sung. Alleluia.'

At the end of the song, Prophet Yohana read a lesson from the holy bible and then told Nene Tsatsu that he had been delivered from the torments of the evil spirit. He assured him that the spirit he was seeing had been made powerless. So he was free to do his normal duties again, and have a sound sleep at night. Then as if he was preaching to him and his people, he told them the driving away of the spirit was not made possible through his own personal power. 'It was through the power of God Almighty who could do anything one asks of him, if only he has faith in Him,' he told them. So he advised them to pray all the time to glorify God and put their petitions before Him and they would not be disappointed.

Before he left the palace, Prophet Yohana invited Nene Tsatsu to a thanksgiving service at his church the following Sunday. He said that would give him the opportunity to worship together with other church members, and show his appreciation to the Lord for what He had done for him.

That night, for the first time in almost a week, Nene Tsatsu had a sound and peaceful sleep. It was a great joy to his wives, and indeed the whole household. And for the first time the chief and his wives prayed together, glorifying God and giving Him thanks for what He had done for the chief. The news of his deliverance soon spread far and wide, and many people were happy that their chief was mentally and emotionally sound again, to continue his normal duties.

The next day which was Sunday, Nene Tsatsu was one of the first worshippers to arrive at the People's Charismatic Church for the thanksgiving service. Before the service started, Prophet Yohana officially introduced him to the congregation and every worshipper was happy the chief had come to fellowship together with them. There was praise and worship, and the giving of testimonies. When Nene Tsatsu gave his testimony, everybody was filled with great joy. More prayers were said and more songs were sung, praising God for His powers over the devil. Nene Tsatsu's attendance of church services at this church became noticeably frequent but he did not sever relations with Christ Church, the church into which he was baptized.

One day, the kingmakers and the royal councilors called on Nene Tsatsu. They were delighted to hear that he slept soundly and had come to express their happiness to him, and brief him on what transpired during the past few days. First they reminded the chief of the land case they were judging before the incident which kept him out of official duties, and informed him that it was peacefully settled. Padi was found guilty, as it was agreed upon, for reselling the piece of land to Atter when he had already sold it to Terku. He was fined one live sheep, two bottles of gin and a cash sum of a hundred pounds. Terku was recognized the legal owner of the land and so Padi was again ordered to refund the money Atter paid to him.

Nene Tsatsu was informed that Akortorku took advantage of his situation to fabricate many stories about him with a view to discrediting him. The councilors also told him about his alliance with the family members of the late Kwam, the secret meetings they had together to plan his removal from the stool, and the meeting with the people of Adoma they were planning to have. Some of the members wanted Nene Tsatsu to give Council members power to stop the meeting his opponents had planned. But he was not in favor of that prevention order which, he said, was not democratic. He told them that in democracy, freedom of gathering and speech was a right and so Akortorku and his plotters should be allowed to have their meetings. He believed that would help the people to take their own decision.

Nene Tsatsu then advised his councilors to exercise restraint and be calm because he did not believe there was any cause for an alarm. He recounted the developments they had brought to the village; including the school block they had put up for their children and the road they had constructed which had changed lives of the people, and said; with those things in view, he was optimistic the people would not support his opponents' selfish unpopular plans.

Chapter 11

When the bunch of conspirators heard of Nene Tsatsu's deliverance, many of them were disappointed. They thought he would continue to be tormented by the evil spirit so that they could use his state of affairs as one of the reasons for his removal from office. However, they decided the meeting with the people should go on as planned. By eight o'clock in the morning, a fairly large number of people had assembled at Laasi Park, and more continued to arrive. That day was a non-farming day and so the opposition members expected a large number of people to be present at the meeting. People were still arriving when the leaders of those opposed to Nene Tsatsu led by Akortorku and Asawatse Kodjo mounted the platform. Akortorku was the first to speak. He began his speech by requesting the people to give him an attention.

'Ago o o o! (May I have your attention, please?)'

Some noise could still be heard in the crowd and so he repeated his call for silence, this time raising his voice higher.

'Ago o oo!'

The second call brought some silence. Akortorku waited for a few seconds and then began to speak:

'My good people of Adoma, my colleagues and I welcome you to this very important meeting. We are very happy to see many of you here. This shows how concerned you are about the appalling things happening in our village. We have called you here today to take an important decision with you. But before we take this decision, you must know why we need a decision to be taken. And so I will like to brief you on some unusual things that are going on in our dear village.'

'What is going on? Tell us, we want to know,' somebody in the crowd asked.

'Well,' Akortorku continued. 'I am sure many of you know that Nene Tsatsu was not, I repeat, was not the person who should have been our chief. But some people ignored our sacred traditional process and decided to make him our chief because of his education, they said.'

'Yes, education makes one more enlightened,' another person interrupted.

'We all thought,' Akortorku went on, 'that in spite of the fact that he was not the rightful person to be the chief, he would try to be an embodiment and custodian of our noble tradition and transact his duties according to our customs. But, my brothers and sisters, we are all disappointed. Instead of sticking to tradition and ruling Adoma as our ancestors had done, he is using his Whiteman's education to do things the way he likes, and lord over…'

'How is he doing that?' another person reacted.

'Most of the time he is not in the palace,' Akortorku continued. 'He is always in the city visiting friends and drinking wine with them, forgetting that he has sacred duties to do as a chief. He has destroyed our farms under the pretext of bringing progress to Adoma. But in fact, he advocated for the rehabilitation of the road so that he could travel smoothly to the city to visit his friends.'

'That is not true. We are all using the road to transport our goods to Kesua,' a man from the crowd reacted. But Akortorku ignored him and went on;

'All along, he has been selfish and partial. You are all aware of how Detse was killed and what happened afterward.'

'But what happened? My brothers and sisters, what happened? May he rest in peace.'

He paused for a while, and since nobody answered his question which was, in fact, rhetorical, he went on:

'Because of Nene Tsatsu's relationship with Detse, he used his influence and stood in the way of justice and now he is scot-free and enjoying perfect life.'

'We cannot continue to serve such a chief, especially when he has now got the sickness of the head because he has offended our ancestors. So we are here today to take a joint decision. We need your support so that we can depose him and replace him with a more matured and traditional person.'

'One thing you must know,' he continued, 'is that the Whiteman's education does not automatically make one a wise man and for that matter, a good ruler. There is a difference between education and wisdom. What we need from a chief is good leadership, and only a man of wisdom can give that to us.'

Akortorku's speech was given a mixed reaction from the people. While some of them shouted: 'No removal from

121

office, we are happy with Nene Tsatsu'; others said, 'we want the rightful person in office.' The last reaction seemed to please Akortorku and so he turned to consult with his colleagues on the stage. Then suddenly, Linguist Nanor unexpectedly appeared, to the astonishment of the people, and even the conspirators.

Linguist Nanor went to the meeting place only to hear what the opposition members would say about Nene Tsatsu. But it reached a stage where he could not contain himself. So he felt he had to speak to defend the chief, damn the consequences. So he mustered courage and mounted the platform in an attempt to counter all that Akortorku had said about Nene Tsatsu.

The organizers of the meeting were unhappy with Nanor's intrusion. They considered his effrontery to join them on the stage an insult. So Akortorku angrily and aggressively moved toward him and asked him to get down. There was a tense moment as the people looked on in anxiety. Nanor refused to dismount. The other people on the stage also moved toward him, obviously to help Akortorku remove him from the stage, physically. The people did not want the confrontation to develop into crisis. That was not what they wanted in Adoma. So one of them shouted:

'Allow him to speak, allow him to speak.' Another person added:

'If he wants to speak, let him do so, we want to hear him too.'

These were followed by other calls asking Nanor to be allowed to speak, some of which were drown by the deafening noise. There was nothing the opposition members could do any more. They still thought they commanded the support of the people and so they did not want any incident to kill that support. So they left him alone on the other side of the platform.

There was still noise going on but Nanor did not want to waste any more time, and so he began to address the people as his opponents look on:

'My dear men and women of Adoma, I greet you all,' Nanor started. 'I am here on my own behalf, not to condemn or judge anybody but to tell you what I know so that you can make your own minds.'

'I heard all that you have been told about Nene Tsatsu, and I am here to let those of you, who are not aware of it know that the decision to have an educated chief was approved by both royal families. My colleague, Akortorku, and some of the people on this platform were parties to that decision. The kingmakers and all of us at the traditional council were in an agreement. And since he became our chief, I do not think Nene Tsatsu has been lacking in his duties. We…'

'No o o o! He is doing well as a chief.' 'Go on, we are listening,' another voice from the crowd was heard.

'My dear people,' Nanor continued, 'our chief is working hard for Adoma. We now have a good school building for our children and a clinic for our minor medical treatments. Most of our women do not carry foodstuffs on their heads to Kesua market anymore because our road is now in good condition. All these developments were made possible because of Nene Tsatsu's wisdom and the love he has for the people of Adoma.'

'In the development of a place, or in life, some people have to make sacrifices for the benefit of others. During the

Kabo wars many of our ancestors sacrificed their lives, and now we are enjoying life. Therefore if some of us have to sacrifice some portions of our lands so that a school could be built or a road could be constructed, I do not think it is too much a price to pay.'

There was another "no o oo!" in agreement with what Nanor had said, and other inaudible responses from the crowd. At this stage, the conspirators realized they were losing the battle. So they started leaving the platform one by one in terrible anger, amidst jeers from the crowd. Eventually, only two members, who were from the late Kwam's family, were left on the platform. Nanor then on:

'Nene Tsatsu is not sick as you have wickedly been told.

Anyone who doubts what I am saying now can go to the palace and find out. I will like to remind everyone that we in Adoma have elders and kingmakers who are traditionally responsible for the choice, installation and deposition of chiefs; and not a group of disgruntled people who are desperate to have Nene Tsatsu removed from office because they do not like him.'

'Nanor ended his speech by reminding the people again of all that Nene Tsatsu had done for Adoma, including the putting up of the school building and the clinic, the construction of the feeder road and the market, and other projects in progress. Then he told them that even though he was the chief, Nene Tsatsu physically participated in most of the projects. Whenever he had no business at the palace, he was either at the work site or in the city appealing to institutions for technical or material assistance for our projects,' he continued. Finally, he advised the people:

'Therefore you must not allow selfish enemies of progress to deceive you and destroy the unity we have in Adoma. I thank you all very much.'

As he dismounted the platform, he could hear reactions from the crowd, such as, 'Traitors,' 'we were deceived,' they misled us,' 'we shall let them pay for their actions'. Nanor went back to the platform and appealed to the people not to take the law into their own hands. Then he finally descended the platform and went away, convinced that he was able to achieve his aim. As he walked away, the crowd moved too, in various directions, and Laasi was left behind. That was the end of Akortorku-organized meeting.

The two elders from the late Kwam's family, who decided not to leave the platform when he was talking to the people, followed him. Nanor wondered why they were following him. They walked faster and soon caught up with him. Then surprisingly they entered into a conversation with him. Initially, he did not show any interest but when he realized they were in a friendly mood, he got interested in what they had to say. The two men thanked Nanor for his bravery in coming to the meeting to give them the real picture of the state of affairs; and apologized to him for joining Akortorku in his opposition to Nene Tsatsu. Then in another surprise move, they promised Nanor that they were going to advise their new leader, Asawatse Kodjo, to respond to the chief's invitation for a peaceful settlement of the rift between them and the chief, as a result of the death of Kwam.

Nanor was very happy to know that there was the possibility of the Sasu people going to the palace to have a dialogue with Nene Tsatsu. He expressed his gratitude to both men, and assured them that he would pass on the information to the Chief.

As soon as the two elders branched to their various homes, Huno and Okete caught up with Nanor. Both councilors were also at the meeting on their own accord. When Akortorku was delivering his speech, they were among the crowd monitoring the reactions of the people. It was when Nanor mounted the platform that they got to know that he, too, was there. Initially, they were filled with fear, and blamed him for taking the risk. But when his reception became positive, their fears were allayed. At the time he left the platform, Huno and Okete were engaged in conversations with some of the people and so they could not leave at the same time Nanor left.

The three councilors discussed the meeting and Huno and Okete praised Nanor for his courage. All of them agreed that the meeting was worth attending. They believed Nanor's speech was able to sway the people away from Akortorku and his group of detractors. When Nanor informed his friends of the assurance the two elders from the late Kwam's family gave him, they were extremely pleased. It was a great opportunity, they agreed, that must be seized immediately to settle the accident case and restore the harmony that was dented. So they decided to head straight to the palace to inform Nene Tsatsu of the great news.

The three men were shocked to find so many people already at the palace. Most of them had come straight from the meeting to reassure Nene Tsatsu of their solidarity and solid support for him. As soon as they saw Nanor, some of them hailed and carried him shoulder high, calling him,

'The true son of Adoma.' Nene Tsatsu was all smiles when he saw him. It was evident that the people, who had arrived earlier, had briefed him on what transpired at Akortorku's abortive meeting. However, Nanor narrated everything to him again, including his conversation with the elders from the late Kwam's family. The chief was full of praises. He congratulated him, Huno and Okete for their courage and fearless defense of what they were doing for the people of Adoma. Then in a short speech, he thanked all the people for the confidence they had in him and the support they were giving him. He assured them that in spite of the unhealthy activities of a few individuals Adoma was going to see more developments taking place.

That night, Akortorku could not have a sound sleep. The continuous thought of the abrupt ending of his meeting with the people, filled him with uncontrollably fury. He put the blame squarely on the organizers, including him, for allowing Nanor to speak.

We should not have allowed Nanor to speak, he thought.

He admitted they made a serious damaging mistake by allowing him to speak which made them unable to achieve their aim.

The following day, he tried to consult with his associates to find a way forward without much success. Most of his supporters, mostly from the late Kwam's family, became disinterested in him. That was a tremendous blow to him because he realized for the first time that he was losing grounds in achieving his objectives. For days, he was unable to go out in public, fearing that the people might vent their spleen on him. The only place he could go to was his corn farm which was not far from his house.

And true to his fears, there were rumors emanating from many sources that a group of people were planning to attack him. When this was brought to the notice of Nene Tsatsu, he asked Nanor to investigate the rumors as soon as possible. That was done and it was found out that the rumors were credible. So Nene Tsatsu requested a general meeting with the people to be arranged at the palace immediately.

Accordingly, the village crier went to all corners of Adoma to summon people to the meeting, beating his gong, for attention. When the time came, a sizeable number of people turned up to hear what Nene Tsatsu had to say. He began his speech by thanking the people for coming to the emergency meeting. Then he continued:

'The events of the last few days,' he continued, 'show that you wholeheartedly embrace and appreciate what we are doing to bring progress to Adoma. This gives me great encouragement and the determination to help you engage in more projects to enhance our village's development.'

'I am so happy you did not allow yourselves to be misled by a few disgruntled people whose aim is just to destroy our unity and derail our progress. Just as we shall not allow anybody or group of people to bully us into changing our course of direction, it is equally proper that we too should refrain from harassing people who might be against us.'

'No o o! They are our enemies, enemies of progress, and so we should let them know that,' a man from the crowd shouted.

'Nobody is an enemy,' Nene Tsatsu went on. 'Some people may not agree with us but that does not mean they are our enemies. In this world, you may not have a hundred per cent of people's backing for something you want to do. That is why there is democracy in which the majority carries the mandate. I know we are in the majority and so once we believe we are doing the right things, nobody can hold us back.'

'I hear there are plans going on to attack some of our brothers. This is not in the spirit of brotherhood and, surely, not in the spirit of our advancement. If what I hear is true, then I advise the planners to refrain from it. That will not advance our progress. This is the main reason why I have called you here. Without peace and unity there will never be progress.'

'I am sure those who do not agree with us have realized their folly by now and are ashamed of themselves. So it will not be long, I sincerely believe, when they will come back to help in our revolution to change the status of Adoma,' Nene Tsatsu concluded.

He took advantage of the meeting to review all the achievements they have made, and said they could not have done all those things without the unity that was then at stake. After that, he invited questions or comments from the people. Many issues were raised and addressed, and then the chief asked Linguist Nanor to brief the people on the next projects to be undertaken.

In his briefing, he told the people that the digging of another well would start on the eastern side of the village as soon as the one on the west was completed. In addition to that, he informed them plans were in progress to construct a market at Adoma. This was greeted with a long applause.

'We believe,' he went on; 'the construction of a market will give us the opportunity to sell most of our foodstuffs here at Adoma. This will relieve us from the stress of transporting everything to Kesua market. Now that our road is in a motor able condition, he reminded them, many traders will be willing to come here to trade with us,' Nanor told the people.

In throwing more light on the envisaged market, Nanor revealed that permission had already been given by the paramount chief and the District Council for the construction of the market to go ahead. Asked where it would be situated, he told them it would be at the very place where their goods were stored before transporting them to Kesua. He added that the place had to be expanded and leveled to allow enough space for sellers and buyers, stalls and kiosks, and a space for drivers to park their vehicles.

Before the meeting ended, Nanor reminded the people of the agreement reached with Nene Tsatsu that there should be no revenge on anyone who disagreed with them or stood against the projects. He told them there were many ways they could guard against the developments taking place without direct confrontation with, or molestation of anybody. So in spite of the fact that some of the people did not agree with what was said about actions being considered against the enemies of the people, they left the meeting pleased with everything discussed. Nene Tsatsu was equally happy with the mood they were in. That made him more determined than ever to carry on with Adoma's transformation.

During the week, another meeting was held. Nene Tsatsu called for this meeting because of the willingness of the late Kwam's family members to have a dialogue with him. He wanted to seize that opportunity to settle the case between them and Detse for peace to prevail. So he was very happy that both parties turned up.

After the normal exchange of greetings, Nene Tsatsu provided drinks, as custom demanded, to welcome the participants. Libation was then poured by Linguist Nanor in which he prayed for peace and good health. Then he asked the ancestors to be present in their midst and guide them in their deliberations. Surprisingly, before Nene Tsatsu was ready to officially open the meeting, an elder representing the late Kwam's family got up and asked permission to speak.

'Nene Tsatsu 111,' he began his speech, 'before you tell us the purpose for which you have invited us here, permit me to say a few words.' Everybody listened to the elder's introductory words with great anxiety and interest.

'We, of the late Kwam's family,' he continued, 'are pleased to inform you that we have a new family leader. We are sorry this has not been done as custom demands until now.'

'Developments after the death of our late leader unfortunately prevented us from coming to introduce our new leader to you earlier. We are very sorry for this. It is unwise to recall the events now. The most important thing is that we are happily here today.' The speaker was given a long applause, followed by a remark from Nanor:

'We are also glad you are here with us.'

'It is now my pleasure to present to you, Nene Tsatsu, our new family leader, Asawatse Kodjo,' the elder ended his speech. The warm reception and the applause given to him was tremendous and very hearty.

In his welcome address, Nene Tsatsu said he was very happy to receive the new leader of the Sasu clan and thanked the elder for his wise words. Then he went on:

'As you rightly said, it will not do us any good to bring back things of the past or to continue to ask why things had to go the way they went. In life, unexpected things are bound to occur and when they do happen people react in various ways. And when this happens; I do not think blames should be apportioned in any way.'

'It is when people begin to take advantage of the unfortunate situation to achieve their own personal and selfish ambition that we should be concerned. I believe the best thing to do is to come together when the unexpected happens and try to find out how to solve the problem, restore peace and how to move forward,' Then turning to Asawatse Kodjo, he said:

'Asawatse Kodjo, you are warmly welcome. I pray that God gives you good health, wisdom and good leadership qualities to enable you lead your people, and the people of Adoma. I hope you will follow the footsteps of your predecessors, and work together with the chieftaincy to develop our village.'

At the conclusion of Nene Tsatsu's welcome address, the elder man of the Sasu people presented him with one live sheep, four bottles schnapps and four bottles of the local gin. This was in connection with the presentation of their leader, Asawatse Kodjo, to him, as custom demanded. The drinks were received by Linguist Nanor on behalf of the chief but they were returned to Nanor to be served to all the people.

While the drinking was going on, Nanor joked that the elder man of the Sasu clan was his friend. When asked how they became friends, he stated that they became friends on the platform at Laasi Park during the Akortorku-organized meeting. Many of them burst into laughter. The elder man himself could not help laughing heartily. That was an apparent reference to the abortive meeting convened by those who were then opposed to Nene Tsatsu. Nanor told his colleagues how happy he was that everything was put behind them to allow peace to prevail.

The presentation of Asawatse Kodjo to Nene Tsatsu was followed by the main business of the day; which was a settlement of the case between the Sasu clan's people and Detse. Painful as it was, Nene Tsatsu appealed to the family members to consider the circumstances in which the late Kwam died, and agree to a peaceful settlement. After other people from both sides had spoken, it was unanimously agreed that the case should be settled out of court.

In his speech that followed the agreement, Nene Tsatsu happily said everybody should be happy with the peace they had renewed; adding that even the spirit of the late Nene Tsatsu 11 would be pleased. He reminded them that even though their ancestors were in the other world, they were still watching over them. And he wondered how their late chief would have felt if they had taken a different course of action. Then he thanked everybody for the various roles they played in the reconciliation of the two families, telling them he believed their actions would make the spirit of their late chief rest in perfect peace.

The family of the late Kwam did not ask for it, but he announced that the palace would pay for all the expenses incurred during his funeral. In addition to that, he informed the family that even though by tradition the late Kwam's wife would be cared for by his junior brother as a husband, any time she was in serious need she could come to the palace for help. He again revealed that he would meet with the elders to decide on a fitting compensation to be paid to Kwam's family for their loss but that was declined by the family elders. Asawatse Kodjo told the gathering that the refusal was in good faith and that the loss was not only for the Sasu clan but also the whole of Adoma. Secondly, he felt the expression of regret and the peace settlement that was put in place were more important than any material compensation.

Then to cement the reconciliation the representatives of both families got up, shook hands and embraced each other. After that, Nene Tsatsu produced two bottles schnapps, two of the local gin, and a very fat sheep to be used as a seal for the peace agreement. Before the drinks were served, and in accordance with custom, Linguist Nanor poured libation, first to thank the almighty God for the peaceful settlement of the case, and then to appeal to the ancestors not to allow any more tragedies to befall them. At the completion of the pouring of the libation, the drinks were served. While drinking was going on, the sheep was slaughtered and prepared. It was then portioned into pieces and everybody present at the meeting was given a piece to take home as prove of the settlement.

Chapter 12

Nene Tsatsu knew that for a community to progress, it was vital that peace and unity must prevail. That was the reason why he was tremendously happy with the outcomes of the peace meetings he had; first with the general public and then with the families of the late Kwam and Detse. The only remaining problem was the one being posed by Akortorku. Even though he was from the other royal family and a member of the Council of elders he had stopped coming to him or attending meetings, and had chosen to wage war on him. But this did not discourage him. He was, as usual, happy to concentrate on his programs, knowing very well that he had solid support from a majority of the people.

One day when he got time to visit the market construction site, he was amazed at the large number of people working, and the great progress made. In order to get the size of land needed for the market, three land owners had to lose parts of their lands. But they did not stand against the acquisition. Two of the three land owners were on site taking part in the construction of the market and Nene Tsatsu had the opportunity to chat with them. Unlike what happened during the construction of the road, the two men told the chief it was a pleasure for them to offer their lands because it would benefit all the people of Adoma. Nene Tsatsu noticed with pleasure that the number of people working on the project had increased. That was because those who hitherto refused to take part in the community work had changed their mind. These people included the Sasu people under Asawatse Kodjo who had renewed their allegiance to Nene Tsatsu, and individual people from Akortorku's family. As a result of this reconciliation with Nene Tsatsu, Akortorku became isolated. He was no more seen in public and nobody knew where he was or what his plans were.

Because of the large number of people taking part in the construction work each working day, the market was completed, ahead of schedule. A neem-tree was planted in the middle as a symbol and then the market was demarcated and the designated spaces were marked for special activities. These included areas for the selling of foodstuffs and European goods. Three small stalls were built; two to be used for storing goods, and the other as a canteen. In addition, two toilet facilities were put up a few meters away from the space allocated for vehicles.

When Nene Tsatsu was satisfied that the whole area was safe, a dedication and opening day was announced at Adoma and Kesua. Guests at the ceremony on that day included officials from the District Council and representatives from the two churches in Adoma. Nene Tsatsu gave a short speech to welcome the guests and then libation was poured to thank the ancestors and ask for their continuing guidance. This was followed by prayers by the two church leaders to similarly express the village's gratitude to God and seek His blessings. Then a white sheep was sacrificially slaughtered to cleanse the place and make it safe for the transaction of business, as tradition demanded.

At the end of the rituals, an official from the District Council addressed the gathering. In his speech, the Chief Executive commended the people of Adoma for their exemplary foresight and self-help spirit which had enabled them to undertake many projects, including the market they were about to dedicate. He noted, with pleasure, that their community spirit and their hard work had transformed the place from a typical village status to one close to a town. He hoped that other villages would learn and emulate the Adoma spirit, and stop asking government for the provision of everything they needed.

Touching on health and safety, the Chief Executive advised the people of Adoma to make hygiene and the safety of everybody their priority, since many people would be coming to the market to do business. In addition, he advised them among other things, that the market should be kept clean and tidy all the times to avoid the spread of diseases. At the end of his speech, he cut the tape to declare the market open. This was followed by fanfares, drumming and dancing which normally characterized such traditional ceremonies. That day was Kesua market day and so many people from the market stopped for a while to partake in the celebration, which lasted for a long time. Even after Nene Tsatsu and the invited guests had left, it still continued.

Nene Tsatsu had two meetings at the palace soon after the opening of the market. The first was with his councilors. It was to reappraise the newly completed projects. Almost all the councilors praised the people for their enthusiasm and the large turnout for the work which sped up the completion of the market. Special gratitude was expressed to the people of the Sasu clan and their new leader, Asawatse Kodjo, who joined the workers after the peace agreement. Nene Tsatsu then gave a short speech:

'As soon as the market is opened for trading on Wednesday,' he informed his councilors, 'the people of Adoma will have a choice to make. The choice will be whether to sell their goods here at Adoma; or to continue to take them to the main market at Kesua, in which case they will have to pay transport costs. But whatever choice they make, I am sure it will make life easier for them,' he concluded. Finally, he thanked his elders for the contribution they were making in transforming Adoma and changing the lives of the people.

The maintenance of the market was then discussed. Nene Tsatsu suggested that it was necessary to have a group of people to be responsible for its running and management. This was unanimously accepted and so a committee of five people was agreed upon. But the selection of those who should be on this committee was to be done by the councilors later, after consulting the people. In selecting the members, Nene Tsatsu advised that two women should be included, and only one councilor should be a member.

Members were also to find out how much toll should be charged in order to raise funds for the maintenance of the market. One day, Nene Tsatsu had another meeting. This time, it was between him and his wives. When he was told that they wanted to have a discourse with him, he wondered why they wanted to see him. He could not remember the last time they came to him together. Occasionally they met at the living room and talked about family affairs, but those meetings were not prearranged. Therefore when he was informed that they wanted to see him together, he kept on thinking of what might have gone amiss. However, he was pleased to meet his wives. It was he who first spoke.

'Actually when I was informed that you wanted to have a meeting with me, I asked myself what had gone wrong. This is because you hardly come to me for a talk together unless I send for you.'

'There is nothing to worry about, Nene,' responded Naki.

'There is something to worry about, Nene, and that is the reason why we are here,' interrupted Abla.

'What is it, then, I am listening,' requested Nene Tsatsu.

'It is all about Akortorku, Nene. We have been monitoring his opposition to you and his utterances in public, and we are not happy with what we hear,' said Abla.

'Yes, Nene, we are concerned about you. You know hatred breeds evil machinations which in most cases result in disastrous consequences. We do not want anything like that to happen to you,' Naki added.

Nene Tsatsu grinned and then told his wives not to worry about Akortorku because he could not do anything against him.

He said he was convinced that the almighty God was satisfied with what he was doing. But Abla warned him seriously not to take what they were telling him lightly. She stated:

'I was born and bred here and have lived here all my life and so I know what I am talking about. I have seen chiefs come and go, some after a short time on the stool. In addition, I know what people like Akortorku can do. He can

139

do anything imaginable to achieve his aim, Nene. That is the reason why we are worried,' Abla concluded.

Nene Tsatsu was quiet for some time. Then he asked his wives what they wanted him to do. So they advised him to be more careful in his dealings with Akortorku, and involve him in all palace activities. This was because they did not often see him taking part in most of the projects. But Nene Tsatsu told his wives he had already involved him in all palace programs. He was a councilor and as a councilor, he was to attend palace meetings and take part in all activities. But he chose not to attend meetings. He went further to tell his wives how he had sent special personal messages to him, through Nanor. But regrettably, Akortorku would not come to the palace.

Abla responded by telling Nene Tsatsu that all he had told them was a proof of the fears they had for him. She asked her husband what he thought Akortorku might be planning to do in secrecy, since he had isolated himself from the palace. That was a question Nene Tsatsu could not answer. So his wives advised him to use everything in his power to win Akortorku's favor again to prevent a possible tragedy. 'Our elders say being circumspect is not a show of cowardice,' Abla reminded Nene Tsatsu. And with this serious advice from her, the family meeting ended.

For days after this meeting, Nene Tsatsu contemplated over the opinions expressed by his wives about Akortorku and decided to act on the advice given him without delay. He was a man who always advised people not to take chances because, according to him, taking of chances normally result in regrettable consequences. So he did not want to take chances himself. But before acting on his wife's advice, he decided to seek more information about the character of Akortorku and what he was really capable of doing. So he invited Linguist Nanor to the palace, hoping that he would get what he wanted to know from him.

Nanor's estimation of Akortorku was not different from what Nene Tsatsu's wives had told him. He said he knew him as a man who always wanted things to be done in his own way. This character of his, he added, had resulted in many conflicts, some of which were acrimonious, between him and a number of people in the village. The chief sat back in his seat and raised his eye brows in shock when Nanor made mention of Akortorku's great interest in black magic.

Nanor told him that Akortorku's name was mentioned in many juju-related incidents in the past. On, at least, one occasion, there was an allegation that he was the cause of a neighbor's death. But he denied it and since nobody was bold enough to prove it, the allegation died a natural death. When Nene Tsatsu asked him to throw more light on Akortorku's interest in juju, Nanor informed him that he had a friend renowned in charms who always came to the village to visit him. Nobody knew how involved he was in the practice himself but one day he was accused of retorting to juju power to achieve his aim when he did not get what he wanted. As a result of this, many people were always careful not to step on his toes.

Nene Tsatsu was satisfied with the information he had about Akortorku. So he asked Nanor to arrange a special meeting with all the councilors to discuss the problem he was posing to him. He also asked him to find out if he could get any level-headed person in Akortorku's family and invite him to the meeting. Personally, he was not worried about what he could do but for the sake of Adoma, he wanted something done immediately to sustain the harmony they were enjoying. He therefore hoped that Akortorku would attend the meeting to tell the council what his problems were so that they could be addressed. 'A doctor cannot prescribe any medicine for a sick person unless he knows the sickness he is suffering from,' he told Nanor. He therefore hoped that Akortorku would be patriotic and sincere enough and cooperate with them so that the right prescription would be made to solve the prevailing problems.

Chapter 13

On the first market day, it was amazing to see many sellers, buyers and people who just came to have a look at the new market. For the first time in the history of Adoma, people saw three parked vehicles waiting to convey traders out of Adoma. Among the people who came to see how trading was going on were Nene Tsatsu and his councilors, and some of the elders in the village. They did not need to go to work because the day was traditionally a non-working day.

The chief took advantage of the occasion to go round and chat with many of the traders to find out their opinions about the novel market. He was glad the people he talked to were happy to have a market at Adoma, and pleased with what he was doing for the people. The traditional council members also went round to sample people's opinions about the market and other developments that had taken place. Like Nene Tsatsu, they too were not disappointed. Some of the people gave suggestions, but on the whole they were unanimously satisfied with the developments going on in the village.

On an occasion like that, people expected Akortorku to be present since he was a member of the traditional council. Even his colleagues expected him to be present. After all, he did not play much role in the construction of the road yet on its opening day, he was one of the men who tried to take the first free ride.

Soon rumors about Akortorku's whereabouts began to spread throughout the village. One was that he had gone to Tapon to visit a relative. And another was that he had left for Damey. It was a confused state of situation but the fact was that Akortorku was not in the village and many people were worried. He was not actually needed very much but people would like to know his whereabouts because of his malicious character. For about a month, nobody had seen him in Adoma.

Then one day, news spread that Akortorku got sick and had been taken to the clinic.

'Did you say Akortorku is seriously ill?' asked a concerned man.

'Yes, this is what I hear,' replied the informant.

'When did he return home to be seriously ill so suddenly?'

'I understand he came back in the evening. His illness started in the night, and in the morning he was taken to the clinic,' the informant added.

For several days, he was detained at the clinic but there was no improvement in his condition. The doctor at the hospital in kesua who occasionally came to work at the clinic did many tests on him but he could not diagnose the sickness. This was a worry to him and Akortorku's relatives. As the news of his sickness expand throughout the village, many people went to the clinic to visit him and wish him speedy recovery. Among the concerned people who visited him were Nene Tsatsu and Linguist Nanor. They

144

were very sorry when they heard of his ill-health and, in spite of his hostile attitudes toward the chief, they went to visit him.

Akortorku's illness was pains in the stomach which made him vomit profusely. As a result, he grew thinner and weaker. When the illness first started, the vomiting was very frequent. In the second week, his relatives took him back home because they considered his illness one that could not be cured with western medicine. So a traditional fetish priest was sent for. When he saw Akortorku on his arrival, he shook his head. He was given a seat but he ignored it and, instead, sat on the floor. Then he opened a black bag he was carrying and brought out some items including cowries.

The juju man shook his head again and said he had seen something, but he would not say anything until what he saw had been confirmed. Before he started divining, he asked whether Akortorku was born on a Wednesday. When his wife answered in the affirmative, he said he knew but he wanted it to be confirmed. He uttered some words which nobody understood, took the seven cowries one by one with his left hand and put them into his right hand. Then he threw them on the floor in front of him. He gathered them, and again threw them on the floor. On the third occasion, he shook his head, the third time he had done so. Those who could read his body movement became alarmed.

At the end of his divination, the juju man posed this question:

'Did he take bush meat on the day he got sick?' Nobody could answer that question apart from his wife. And so she responded: 'Yes, I served him with grass-cutter meat soup which I cooked before he came back home.'

'Ah!' exclaimed the juju medicine man. 'He is not to take bush meat,' he revealed. Akortorku's wife was shocked to hear that because she always cooked bush meat for her husband whenever she got some to buy. So she reacted:

'But that was not the first time he ate bush meat.'

'You do not understand, woman. He is not to take it. This is one of the conditions he was given which he agreed to adhere to,' said the juju man.

'He is not to take the meat of an animal killed with a gun,' the medicine man revealed. He divined again to be doubly sure of what he had found. Then he told Akortorku's people that he made a vow not to eat bush meat and he failed to stick to it, hence his illness. He advised them to take him to the people to whom he made the vow because the illness was beyond his power; adding, 'Maybe they would be able to help him.'

His wife broke down and wept profusely. She bought the meat from the market and used it to prepare palm nut soup. When her husband returned home that evening, he served him with the soup because she did not know about the vow. If he had told her about it, she would not have served him with the soup.

'Oh! Why did he not tell me he was not to eat bush meat when I served him?' she cried out bitterly again. A friend who was filled with pity took her aside in her hands to console her.

'What is the vow for and where was it made?' asked a family member.

'Yes, that is very important to us,' added another man.

'I cannot answer that question,' the juju man replied. Then he added, 'He is now alive and can talk. Ask him to

146

confess and be regretful for what he had done and then, probably, the fetish people there will be able to save him when you get there,' he advised. With this, he packed all his things and went away without demanding any money.

When he left, the people persuaded Akortorku to tell them why he took the vow so that his life could be saved, as the man said. And so after a few minutes of persuasion and with some difficulty, he opened up and told the people everything that took place:

'You know I was not in favor of Nene Tsatsu being made our chief,' he began feebly. The whole place became very quiet because everyone was anxious to hear from him.

'My doubts about him and my dislike for him became justified when he began doing things the way he wanted, and not according to our traditional practices. When he decided to protect Detse from facing the law when he killed Kwam, my hatred for him intensified. So I joined up with members of Kwam's family to find a way to have him deposed.' The place was dead quiet and everyone listened in amazement.

He paused for a while as if he was trying to find out what to say next, or how to say it. The people looked on in astonishment. One of them urged him to continue to speak.

'My anger became more intensive,' he continued, 'when Nanor came to break the meeting we were having with the people. And when I heard that the Sasu people had reconciled with Nene Tsatsu, I decided to take an action alone. So I...' At this stage, he coughed repeatedly. Water was brought to him to drink which he did laboriously. There was quiet for some time. The people did not know what to say. All that they could do was to exchange glances in dismay. After some time, he was prompted to continue what he was saying. So he went on:

'So I decided to get rid of Nene Tsatsu.'

The onlookers screamed loudly but they were asked to stop the screaming and not to say anything until Akortorku had finished with his confession. Then he was asked to continue to speak.

'I therefore went to the azuya cult at Damey and asked for a powerful charm that I could use to get rid of Nene Tsatsu.' The people screamed again in disbelief.

'A charm was prepared for me,' he continued, 'which I was to bury in the palace compound on my return, and then on his next birthday, he would go to join his ancestors.' There was a shout of condemnation from the onlookers. 'But then,' he went on, 'I was warned not to eat the meat of any animal killed with a gun which means I had to refrain from eating bush meat. I made the vow before I accepted the charm and I was to inform my wife about it immediately I got home. But I forgot to do so. Now I hear the meal I took on my return, contained bush meat. Oh! I am so sorry,' he concluded and then burst into tears, joined by his wife and some of his relatives.

Everybody was utterly shocked to hear the unbelievable revelations from Akortorku's own mouth. Some of them did not know whether to sympathize with him in his condition or with Nene Tsatsu, who was the target. Luckily there was a man who knew the juju fetish men Akortorku talked about. So he volunteered to take him and his people there as advised by the fetish priest. Asked where the talisman prepared for him was, he told them it was in a small bag in his room. So the people were asked to take it along with them.

By the next day, the news of Akortorku's evil machinations spread throughout the village. Men discussed it in absolute shock, women gossiped about it in anger, and children relayed it from one place to the other. Those who were not following his activities were surprised to hear what he had planned to do, and those who knew him were amazed that he could go that far. This explained why many people were not very sympathetic with him even though he was unlikely to recover from his sickness. Sympathy was felt rather for Nene Tsatsu, the target of his evil deeds.

Before Linguist Nanor got to the palace to break the sad news to him, people had already thronged his residence. While some of them had come to sympathize with him, others were there to congratulate him on what they considered a narrow escape. They believed God, the Almighty, had saved him from a possible death and so thanks should be given to Him. Some of the people did not come to the palace empty-handed. They brought with them all kinds of drinks, including the native drinks, namely, palm-wine, akpeteshie, and schnapps. Others brought tins of Talcum powder and a live sheep. The powder was sprinkled on Nene Tsatsu as a sign of victory over Akortorku's evil deeds, and the live sheep was kept in the palace to be sacrificed to the ancestors later to thank them for protecting the chief from a likely death.

On this occasion, there was no traditional formality. Nene Tsatsu shook hands and chatted with everybody without his linguist's interpretation. After some time, he whispered something into Nanor's ear. Then he called for silence so that he could pour libation to thank the ancestors for the protection given to the chief. When he got the attention he wanted, he moved a few steps away from the chief, lowered his cover-cloth down to his waist and tightened it firmly. Then he was given a glass into which a little bit of schnapps was poured. He raised the glass of schnapps up and then started pouring the libation in which he praised and thanked the ancestors for the blessings and protection they were giving the chief and the people of Adoma.

In his speech that followed the libation, Nene Tsatsu thanked all the people for the concern and love they had for him.

'I am very grateful to you all,' he went on, 'for your solidarity and support. Our being here today shows that we have been very honest and sincere in the execution of our duties; otherwise, the gods would not have been on our side. As we celebrate my…or our second birth, we must do it without malice or hatred for anybody.'

'We should not even wish those who have planned to destroy us any evil. So let us wish everybody well and carry on with our programs in our desire to help ourselves and our village. Therefore, let us wish Akortorku well and pray for his recovery.'

'I am informed that he went all the way to Damey to purchase a charm which he was to use to kill me. I do not know what he wanted to kill me for. All that we are doing is for the good of Adoma, and I am sure you have all seen the results of the work we have done. Akortorku sees things differently but we must not condemn him.'

'My fellow people of Adoma, one thing we must bear in mind is that our ancestors are always behind us if we do the right things. So the fact that they have blown this evil wind away from us shows that we are on the right path. It is my hope that Akortorku will be able to retrace his steps and disentangle himself from the web which he himself has woven, and come back to join us.

My brothers and sisters, let us take this appalling situation as a lesson to all of us, and try to love one another and eschew hatred and divisiveness. Our aim is to live as brothers and sisters and work harmoniously to make Adoma a comfortable place to live in. I thank you very much.'

Nene Tsatsu's speech was given a long approbation. In their response, the people reiterated their belief in and unflinching support for him. Then he gave all the drinks presented to him to Nanor to be served to all the people.

For days following this, Akortorku was the subject of discussions all over Adoma. Almost everyone condemned him for what he had tried to do. However, it was the hope of everybody that his juju men would be able to save him.

While Adoma waited for news from Damey, the people went about their duties as usual. A request that Nene Tsatsu made to the District Supervisor of schools for the building of a Middle school block attached to the primary school, was granted. That was good news for all parents. Their children could have both stages of their education in Adoma; and go out of the village only when they reached the secondary school stage.

Work on the building started immediately. This time, arrangements for materials were not made by Nene Tsatsu alone. In addition to money contributions that the people decided to make, some individuals donated various kinds of materials. Those who had storekeeper friends in the city and bigger towns brought bags of cement and corrugated iron roofing sheets as donations. The local saw-millers donated plywood and planks while others brought foodstuffs to be cooked for the workers. Jars of the local palm-wine, and bottles of gin, akpeteshie, were brought by the local tappers and distillers as added stimulant to the workers.

Every working day, the attendance at the work site was very high. Only a few people were noticeably absent, mostly the few supporters of Akortorku. They could not be found in the village either. Obviously they had gone underground to escape the shame brought by him and avoid the people's wrath.

The granting of the permission to build the Middle School block came at the end of the academic year. This meant that the building had to be completed before the next academic year so that the graduates from the primary school could stay on and have their middle school education at the village instead of going to Kesua. The work therefore was a race against the three-month long vacation period. Whenever Nene Tsatsu had no official duties to perform at the palace, he was at the work site to give a helping hand. This time, everybody had got to know him and so there were no more raised eye brows or tattling whenever he picked a shovel or a piece of wood. Nene Tsatsu also found time to visit elders in the village. These visits brought the people closer to him and bridged the gap between them and the palace.

His first visit after Akortorku's drama was very beneficial. Everywhere he went, the support and solidarity shown to him was overwhelming. He was satisfied with the conditions of the already completed projects he visited. He took advantage of his presence at one of the work sites to chat with some of the people he met and he was pleased they were happy with the changes taking place. At the clinic, Nene Tsatsu found out that patronage had increased tremendously. That was evidence of the fact that the people were beginning to have faith in health education, and the potency of western medicine. And he was profoundly pleased indeed.

Hitherto, the situation was different. Even some months after the completion of the clinic, many people still preferred traditional herbal treatment to western medicine. Even in the most serious cases they would not be bothered to go to a hospital unless forced to. The mere mention of a hospital always put fear into them. As for the taking of an injection, the lesser it was mentioned the better.

There was the case of an elderly man who was seriously sick for a long time. All this time, he was dependent only on traditional herbal treatment. There was no improvement in his condition, yet he refused to be taken to the hospital at Kesua until his son in the city became fed up with him. One day, he came down and forcefully took him to the hospital. This was very timely because the doctor who treated him told his son that if he had delayed a little longer his father would have died. When this man finally recovered and he was told about what the doctor said, he was grateful. This incident and the health education program Nene Tsatsu introduced in the village when he became chief helped to generate the people's faith in western medicine. That was the reason why attendance at the clinic started increasing remarkably.

Work progressed on the Middle School block steadily, and by the time schools reopened for the next academic year, it was partially completed. An examination was conducted in terms of health and safety and it was certified that the building was safe to be used while the finishing touches were made. Three days before the ceremony to hand over the school building to the district Supervisor of schools, Nene Tsatsu was informed that some members of the opposing royal family of which Akortorku was a member, would like to call on him. He could not believe his ears. For hours, he tried in vain to find out the possible reason for the visit. 'Was he dead?' He asked rhetorically.

No. He gave up that idea because he did not want him to die. He wanted him to recover from his sickness and learn a lesson from what he had tried to do. He thought of other possible reasons and decided that whatever reasons the visit would be he would use the opportunity to try again to restore good relations between the two royal families. So Nene Tsatsu asked Linguist Nanor to invite all the traditional councilors and clan leaders to the meeting.

When it started, it was Goku who first spoke:

'Nene Tsatsu, fellow councilors and elders,' he began his speech, 'I am sure most of you are surprised that we are here to have a meeting with you today. I am saying this because of the unfortunate events following Nene's installation which culminated in unfortunate actions taken by Akortorku.' Some councilors turned their heads and exchanged glances.

'It all started,' he continued, 'after the decision was taken to have an educated chief which changed our traditional pattern of choosing our chiefs. Some of us felt cheated, deprived of our traditional rights and tried to discredit Nene. As if that was not enough, it has now come to light that Akortorku had made an attempt on the life of Nene, to the dismay of all of us.' At this stage, all the people glanced at Nene Tsatsu trying to find out how he would react. But he showed no emotion.

'We are all very happy indeed that the attempt on him was unsuccessful,' Goku went on. 'It was a wicked thing Akortorku tried to do and all of us condemn it. He should not have even thought of it at all. Therefore, the purpose of our visit today is two-fold. We are here to express our sincere sorrow and apology to Nene for the attempt on his life, and then to pledge our full support for him and all activities of the palace. Henceforth, we shall cooperate with him to maintain peace and harmony in our village, and bring progress to Adoma.'

There was a prolonged applause from both the hosts and visitors. Evidently everybody was happy with the change of heart and attitude shown, and pleased with the realization that unity was a prerequisite necessity for the development of Adoma.

'To show that our word is our bond,' he went on, 'we are presenting Nene with four bottles of schnapps and a live sheep to seal our allegiance to him. We hope he will accept them wholeheartedly. Thank you all.' Goku concluded his reconciliatory speech.

Nene Tsatsu accepted the presents wholeheartedly, and then in his response to Goku's speech, he said:

'I wish to say that today is a Christmas day for me, a day I have been yearning for months, and I am elated that it has come at last. You are all warmly welcome.'

'I have noted with pleasure all that you have said and I will like to say that you have done the right thing by coming to have a discourse with us. It is helpful to be in dialogue than to be in confrontation.'

'I noticed a long time ago that something was wrong, that some people were unhappy. And every day, I wondered why the people concerned could not come to me or to any of the councilors for a redress of their grievances. I hear of things they have tried to do or said about me, and I always wondered why they are unable to come to me directly to sort things out.'

'In fact, the things I hear and the actions I am always told about could put one's heart in his boot and unnerve him. But I am not worried because I know that the things we are doing are in the interest of the people.'

'As human beings we are liable to have problems with each other. But when they do happen, and for the sake of fraternity, we have to meet with the person we have the problem with and clear the situation together. I expected a dialogue like this but it did not happen. Nobody came to tell me or any of the councilors what he thought was wrong and how it could be put right. Even when I personally requested it there was no acknowledgement of receipt. Those who have palace duties relinquished them and chose to wage war on me and the palace.'

'You made mention of a decision to have an educated chief but I was not party to that decision. It was the royal families' own decision and upon that you chose to make me your chief. Therefore, I do not think I should be the subject of any grievances.

'One thing I have noticed with our own people is that they criticize a leader not because of breaking rules or poor performance, but out of envy and rancor. Even in our central government, this happens sometimes. But this does not happen very much in western governments, or in organizations I have been associated with. The reason is that it is counter-productive. Theirs is constructive criticism and after this, the opposing members could sit at a table and drink beer together. They are not enemies. This is the secret reason why those in the west are more advanced in many areas of development.'

'Man should be able to develop his environment and make it a comfortable place to live in peacefully. If he is unable to do this, then wherein lays the difference between him and the lower animals? We should try to live up to our role as paragons of virtue and creativity, and live together in harmony.'

'Therefore, if we want Adoma to progress and come closer to the status of a town, then we have to eschew hatred, sectionalism and backbiting. We have to erase all these cankers from our society and work in cooperation with one another. It is only when we do this that can realize our aspirations.'

'Now that it seems we have realized this need, we have a good reason to be happy. With unity and dedication, I am optimistic that we can transform Adoma into a modern town. Once again, I thank you all for what we have achieved today. I am sure our ancestors will be pleased with our realization that unity is fundamentally necessary in a society's progress.'

Nene Tsatsu was given a long spontaneous ovation at the end of his speech. One thing which was noticeable was that he did not mention the name of Akortorku or anyone connected with the opposition against him. When the applause ended, he asked Nanor to bring two bottles of schnapps and a bottle of the local gin, akpeteshie. Together with the drinks presented to him earlier, they were served to everybody. While the drinking was going on, informal discussions concerning the development of Adoma were held. All of them agreed that more still had to be done if they really wanted the village to be a convenient place to live in.

Chapter 14

When everybody had left the palace, Nene Tsatsu thought over the meeting he had with Akortorku's people again. He was not absolutely sure whether the idea of coming to reconcile with him was a camouflage or a genuine change of heart and attitude. So he gave himself time to study the situation. With the help of some of the councilors, he decided to follow the movements of the elders, paying particular attention to their utterances and participation in the community projects.

He expected them to be present at the dedication of the just completed Middle School building and he was pleased to see some of them among the large number of people present. The Supervisor of schools from the district Department of Education was one of the invited guests. He paid a glowing tribute to Nene Tsatsu and the people of Adoma for their foresight and the developments they were bringing to the village. He made them know that their hard work would not be in vain because the Ministry of Education would take over from where they had reached. He promised that all necessary materials would be supplied to keep the school running, and he would make sure that good teachers were provided. Everybody was very happy that day but the happiest were the graduates from the primary school who would have continued their education at Kesua. The completion of the school block was timely for them because it saved them from the hassle of trekking daily to the school.

After the dedication of the school, Nene Tsatsu got the feedback he expected to get from his councilors, and he was extremely pleased. When he became totally satisfied that the pledge to him was, indeed, in good faith, he decided to start arrangements for a major project for the village; something he had been thinking of for a long time. At the lowlands of Adoma were deposits of diamond and gold which the local people were dredging without proper management, using crude methods. The area covered three family lands to the south, including lands belonging to Akortorku's family. Nene Tsatsu wanted the mining to be done on commercial basis but in a manner that what happened during the diversion of the road would not occur again. So now that peace had been restored, he decided to convene a meeting of all the clan heads so that he could put his plans before them.

At the meeting, Nene Tsatsu reminded the elders of the mineral deposits, which most of them were aware of, and told them about the benefits Adoma could get if mining was managed very well. He believed proper mining of the diamond would help accelerate the development of the village and bring jobs to the people. This was discussed, and after weighing the pros and cons, it was unanimously agreed that Nene Tsatsu should be allowed to go ahead with his plans. He was mandated by the elders to officially inform the local government about the economic potentialities of the area and the need for immediate prospecting. Nene Tsatsu was also asked to make mention of the Koro hills which were suspected to be rich in clinker during his meeting with the government officials.

In addition to the discussions the elders had on the economic potentialities of Adoma, they also deliberated on the provision of more social amenities. Many suggestions were made and at the end two things were agreed upon to be provided as a matter of priority. These were the extension of the electric power supply to the southern part of the village and the acquisition of a corn mill to be installed at the market.

While the extension of the power supply would benefit a great number of people, the corn-mill, it was hoped, would hugely be welcomed by the women. It would save them from going to Kesua all the time to mill, especially corn for the preparation of porridge and banku. In order to raise funds for the purchase of the corn-mill, it was decided that households should be made to contribute an equal amount of money. That amount of money was, however, left in the hands of a committee which was formed to make arrangements for the purchase of the corn-mill.

Just before the meeting ended, Akortorku's younger brother and another relative arrived. They were informed on their arrival home from Damey that their elders were at a meeting with the chief and so they went to the palace to see them there. The shocking news they brought was that Akortorku had passed away.

'Did you say Akortorku is dead?' Three of the elders asked simultaneously. Everybody was gripped with grief to the point of weeping. They could not believe what they had heard. For some minutes following the information, nobody could utter a word. They were so shocked that they could not say anything. Some of them could be seen shaking their bent-down heads in disbelief. After some time, one of the elders managed to ask whether Akortorku died before they got to the fetish priests.

They were told he did not die on the way but his illness continued to deteriorate. He complained bitterly of terrible stomach pains and he tried to vomit several times but nothing came out of his mouth. However, they were able to reach Damey but then they had to wait for a whole day because the juju men were out on a mission. When they returned, they consulted with their fetish immediately. This lasted for quite a long time to the displeasure of the people who were greatly worried about his deteriorating condition. They gave him some concoction to drink and waited for a few minutes to work. But there was no reaction from him and no change in his condition.

After that, they had a consultation with their gods for a long time, hoping that they would 'temper justice with mercy' and nullify Akortorku's vow, as it was sometimes the case. When that did not happen, the juju men said because it was a long time since he ate the meat, there was only one more thing they could do to save him. And that was one of them would eat some of the bush meat in the name of Akortorku. That would help them to spiritually remove the effects of the meat from him. Then they asked his people whether they had brought with them the left-over soup or meat he ate.

But Akortorku's people did not know that would be needed. Some of the soup was left after he had eaten but the children ate it the following day. This heart-breaking development intensified the anguish his people were going through. It also forced the juju men to frantically try to find another way of saving Akortorku's life. While still in the process of doing this, Akortorku screamed loudly and unfortunately passed away.

Such an unnatural death, according to custom, was abominable and so his body could not be released to the family. This was because unnatural deaths were considered a curse by the gods and so the dead were not given the normal funeral ceremonies. Rituals had to be performed by fetish priests and the body buried by them. Therefore the juju men felt it was unwise to release the body since they were the very people who could perform the rituals and bury him. Accommodation was therefore found for those who accompanied him so that they could be present at the performance of the rituals and the burial. That was why they could not come back early enough with the news of Akortorku's death. At the end of the information, all the people at the meeting broke down, some of them almost in tears. A relative exclaimed, 'Oh! Akortorku, what have you done to us?'

When those who brought the sad news left, Goku, one of the elders representing his clan was the first to speak. In his lamentation, he spoke of his terrible shock to hear Akortorku was dead and stated that it was a death that should not have occurred. He was aware of how bitter he was about things which, according to him, were going out of traditional order. But he did not have the slightest idea that he was planning something evil, to the extent of trying to destroy Nene's life which had ended in his own death.

On behalf of the family, he apologized to Nene Tsatsu, and revealed that the family would meet later on to think of what to do to move both the family and the entire village forward. Personally, he considered Akortorku's action very worrying and disgraceful. As an elder from a royal family, he should not have dreamt of the action he took.

By taking that action, he had brought a double shame to the entire clan; the shame of trying to kill the chief of Adoma, and one brought to himself by his despicable death. Goku was disturbed that it would not be long when people in the whole district would know about his evil deeds. And since the normal funeral ceremonies could not be performed in his honor, he was fearful even the ancestors would be crossed with him and reject him from their midst.

At this stage, Nene Tsatsu offered his heartfelt condolences to everybody, especially members of Akortorku's family. He said he was shocked to hear of how things happened so rapidly, resulting in his death. Then he told the elders it was not a sad day for members of his family alone but for the whole of Adoma. So at an appropriate time, he would meet all the members again to find out what changes could be made to some of their traditional practices. He therefore closed the meeting so that the family members could return home and mourn the death of Akortorku.

He was however aware no formal rituals or mourning should be organized since his death was a cursed one. If that was done, it would incur the wrath of the gods but Nene Tsatsu wanted a way in which he could be remembered. He genuinely wanted that to be done, at least, in a low-keyed moderate way as an honor to him. Akortorku's aim was to remove him from the stool by killing him, and it was just by the grace of God that the charm backfired. But Nene Tsatsu was not worried about the fact that he was the target. He did not even mention it in any of his speeches and neither did he show any ill-feeling. For this show of maturity and love, many people admired him highly.

Nene Tsatsu bid farewell to the clan leaders but asked the councilors to remain for an unscheduled meeting. When all the clan leaders and elders had left, he was the first to speak.

'I know we have been sitting down for a long time already,' he began, 'but I will like you to wait for a few more minutes so that we can discuss Akortorku's tragic death and pay tribute to him. As you are aware, he was one of us and whatever the case, we should be sorry for him.'

'Excuse me, Nene,' one of the councilors got up to speak.

'Since the time we were informed about Akortorku's death, I have been expecting Nene to show some happiness. But I am surprised that he has so far been indifferent.' Nene Tsatsu turned sharply and looked at him intently. Another councilor asked him what he wanted Nene Tsatsu to be happy about.

Then the councilor continued:

'For a long time, Akortorku had been opposing everything Nene would say or do. That could be ignored but to go to the extent of procuring a charm to be used to kill Nene is, to me, something which should not be taken lightly. It is just by luck that he is alive now. The gods wanted him to live long. That is the reason why Akortorku forgot to tell his wife that he was not to eat bush meat. It was the gods who confused him and made him to forget. Therefore Nene should be pleased that he has had his own death,' he ended his speech.

The second person to speak was Linguist Nanor. He vehemently disagreed with the opinion expressed by his fellow councilor. He told members that if anybody should say anything, favorable or otherwise about Akortorku, then he was the one. That was because he was the only one who knew him more than anybody as a result of the many interactions he had with him. He narrated the many occasions, some of which Nene Tsatsu was already aware of, on which Akortorku expressed his dislike for him, even before he was crowned. Therefore it was not a surprise that he wanted to destroy Nene Tsatsu.

That notwithstanding, he did not think Nene Tsatsu, or any member of the council, should bear him a grudge or rejoice over his death. He concluded by reminding his colleagues that there was only one death, and so regardless of the circumstances leading to the death, he should be mourned. Their chief agreed with what he had said and thanked him for his submission.

Then in response to the views expressed by the other councilors, he told the them that he heard about all the negative things Akortorku said about him, and his avowed aim to remove him from office. He was also aware of his last attempt to kill him which culminated in his own death. But personally, he had no ill-will against him. That was why even though he vacated his post as a councilor, he still considered him as a valued member of the Council. So on several occasions, he sent Nanor to him to find out what his grievances were, and to ask him to come to the palace for a dialogue.

Of course he did not come back but he stressed that that did not mean they should hate him. He added that it was not helpful to bear a grudge against anyone because of what he was, what he stood for or what action he decided to take. He made them understand that human rights entitled one to express his opinions freely. Those opinions might be contrary to theirs, but they did not have to hate one for expressing them. Therefore, he would like everyone to forgive Akortorku for all that he had done. Finally, Nene Tsatsu reminded the councilors:

'We cannot reconcile with him since he is now in the other world. But we have already done so with his clan members, and so we shall use this reconciliation as a bond to work together. I always say that together, we can transform Adoma into a modern town where people will like to live happily.'

Many other councilors expressed their opinions which were not different from what Nene Tsatsu had said. At the end, it was unanimously agreed that a palace delegation should be sent to Akortorku's people to express the palace's sympathy and condolences to the family. According to custom, four bottles schnapps and two bottles of the local gin were made available to the delegation for presentation to the family. Nene Tsatsu was of the hope that the gesture would cement the peace and reconciliation accord which they had entered into with the family.

Chapter 15

The years following the peace agreement and reconciliation with Akortorku's royal family found Adoma in a renewed awareness. There was the realization that without peace and harmony in the village, the progress the people badly needed could not be achieved in the pace they wanted. Enthusiasm and the passion for community work grew very high, and Nene Tsatsu got the cooperation he needed. Every working day, many people turned up to work on the community projects being embarked upon. There was individual dereliction of duty and the flouting of traditional norms anyway, but reasonable peace prevailed. This accelerated work on the projects and the provision of more social amenities for the people.

As usual, Nene Tsatsu had time to visit the project sites to monitor progress and the community cohesion he wanted to exist in the village. Reports reaching him indicated that his delegation to the late Akortorku's family was accorded a warm welcome and that the members were glad to be present at the private funeral.

From the traditional cases he presided upon since he became chief of Adoma, Nene Tsatsu realized that the people's strict adherence to some of their customs and traditional practices was damaging them and the society as a whole. He discovered that some of the practices were placing impediments in the way of community cohesion, social and economic development. So all a long he had been thinking of a reformation of the practices in question, and how his people would take it if he started it. He knew it was going to be a herculean task for him but he was determined to pursue it. His only problem was when to start the reforms, and the thought of how the people would receive the changes. So he decided to shelf his plan until the best opportunity arose.

A year after the death of Akortorku, the normal traditional one-year ritual was privately performed for the peaceful rest of his soul. In normal circumstances, and considering the fact that he was from a royal family, a very big funeral ceremony should have been held in his honor. But because of the belief that an unnatural death was an abomination, and that anyone who suffered such a death was not to be given any formal honor that could not be done. Nene Tsatsu was of the opinion that that belief, and other traditional practices he was aware of, should not be allowed to continue to control people's lives. With that at the back of his mind, he decided time was right for him to advance his course for reforms.

Before he became chief, Nene Tsatsu was made to understand that he was not the one in line to be chief. He was chosen ahead of the rightful person, he was told, because of his education. This, to him, meant that the people saw some good things in an educated person; or in him, in particular, which they would like to make use of. Therefore he expected them to accept and embrace any changes that he would like to bring for the benefit of the society.

So he convened a meeting of all clan leaders and elders so that he could put his concerns and plans before them for a debate. Luckily for him, the meeting was well attended. That was an indication of how committed the people were. Nene Tsatsu opened proceedings by thanking the elders for their presence. Then he continued:

'For Adoma to develop to the status we would like it to be, cooperation and the spirit of community work are very essential. And I am glad to say that from what we have achieved so far, it is evident that we are not lacking in these spirits. But we can do more if we do not allow situations or practices to give cause to disagreements, squabbles and disharmony in the society. In fact, this is the reason why I have called for this meeting.'

'But before we go on with the main discussion, there is something I will like to know,' Nene Tsatsu continued. 'I was told you had to change the rule governing the choice of a chief in order to make me your chief. But nobody told me why you chose me as your first educated chief. Therefore, my elders, if you can tell me your reasons for choosing me, I will be very grateful.'

All the elders turned their heads and glanced at each other, as if they were trying to find out who was the best person to answer the question. Linguist Nanor got up and said that the best person to respond to Nene Tsatsu's question was senior kingmaker, Huno, and so he politely asked him to do so. In his response, he told the chief that since time immemorial, they had been following mainly the traditions laid down for them by their ancestors. But then the white people came to their land with their education, and some of their people, like him, decided to go to their schools to get more knowledge.

What they realized was that some of the new knowledge the educated people acquired were immensely different from what their ancestors had taught them. Again, from what they had seen and heard from other parts of the country, institutions headed by educated people or villages ruled by educated chiefs were developing faster than those governed by illiterates. They thought over those amazing performances and came to the conclusion that the educated rulers were performing better because of the fact that they had two types of knowledge: one from the ancestors and the other from the schools they went to. They believed the combination of the two types of knowledge was the secret behind their wonderful performances.

The people of Adoma wanted developments; kingmaker Huno went on, the kind of developments they had seen in other villages and towns where the rulers were educated people. So the leaders of the various clans met and decided that, for the first time, they would like to have an educated chief who would combine the two types of knowledge to bring developments to the village. But in order to do that, they had to change the traditional guiding rule, and they were happy that they were able to do so peacefully.

As to why they chose him, in particular, to be their chief, kingmaker Huno told Nene Tsatsu that in the first place he was from a royal family, born and bred in the village. Secondly, they believed that he was the only one who would be able to help bring the progress they needed.

Before he took his seat, Huno asked his colleagues if any of them had anything else to add to what he had told the chief. In his contribution, Okete, the other kingmaker, emphasized that Nene Tsatsu's choice was a decision taken by all the elders, and stressed that they believed he could help them bring progress to the village because of his knowledge and experience.

Obviously Nene Tsatsu was very happy with what he had been told. It was just what he expected to hear. Like a school teacher looking for a subject with which to introduce a new topic, he was all the time thinking of how to put his intended traditional beliefs and practices reforms to his people. And so since they made him a chief because they wanted progress in the village, as he was told, he felt he would not have much opposition in telling them about his traditional reforms.

He thanked the elders for the confidence they had in him, and praised them for their foresight. Then he revealed that it was because of the very aims and aspirations they expressed that he called for the meeting. 'You may be right to say educated people are more likely to perform better than those who are not,' he continued and then started to educate his people:

'Western education broadens people's minds by giving them the opportunity to study many subjects and new things different from what our ancestors taught us. The great knowledge that they acquire in school equips them with many ideas. So when they want to do something or are confronted with problems in life, they get solutions faster than those who did not go to school. This is because they have a large stock of ideas from which to look for the best ways to do things or solve problems.'

'They do not depend on the same practices or traditions all the time, whether they are relevant or not. And because of the many ideas they have acquired, they are able to change and keep abreast with the changing trends in the world. This is one of the reasons why western countries are more developed than countries in our parts of the world.'

'What is happening in our world is that we do not change fast enough. We still depend on the same practices or ideas our ancestors brought about ages ago. These practices which we call traditions must have helped our ancestors at the time. But some of them may not be relevant now because the world is changing fast, and so is society. Some may be impediments in our progress and so may not manure the ground for us to sow new ideas. As a result, we are unable to keep pace with the progress going on in other parts of the world.'

Asked what should be done to pave the way for the social and economic developments that were badly needed in Adoma, Nene Tsatsu told his elders that that was something they had to think about together. But so far as he was concerned, all their traditional practices needed to be re-examined. And those that were not favoring and enhancing social and economic advancement should be modernized or abolished.

At this stage, one of the elders asked Nene Tsatsu if he had in mind any traditional practices that he thought were posing problems in the society. This question was welcomed by almost all the elders. The chief said that was a good question in his response but he told the councilors that the purpose of their meeting was not to criticize or condemn outright the traditions instituted by their ancestors. Rather, he went on, they were to find out if they were still relevant to modern society and its advancement. Then he continued:

'I think you are in a better position to know the traditions that are still helping modern society to move forward and those that are retarding progress. This is because you have lived with these traditions and practiced them over a longer period of time than me. But if you want my opinion first, I will gladly tell you what I have noticed.' He went on:

'Since I became your chief, I have been talking with people to find out how they feel about our traditional practices and beliefs, and the roles they are playing in our development. The community projects we are undertaking have given me the opportunity to meet and talk to many people on this matter. And the general opinion expressed by the people I talked to is that some of our traditional practices are retarding the progress of our society. I wish to let you know that I agree with them.'

'One of the people I talked to spoke intelligently, and I found him to be a man of great wisdom. Jokingly, I said to him that he should have been sent to school to be educated. But he told me that would have been impossible because he is a first-born, and that first-borns are not supposed to be sent to school, according to tradition. I was shocked to hear people still believe in this tradition. His explanation was that first-borns are to stay on the land so that when their parents leave to join their ancestors, they could easily take over the lands and other responsibilities.'

'This is one of the traditional practices I am concerned about. Our ancestors instituted this tradition because in their time farming was the main profession; the main source of their livelihood. Now, with the advent of science and technology, there are many professions that people can go into. But in order to gain access into these professions one has to go to school. With the intelligence I noticed in that man, he could have been a great teacher, a lawyer or a doctor, or even a great farmer if he were sent to school. This man could have come back to his society after his education to help in its development. So you see, my elders, our strict adherence to this particular tradition has prevented one, who could have been an asset to the society, from getting educated. We therefore need to think about it seriously.'

'The second tradition to be considered is that of an arranged marriage which includes the marriage of a stool wife.' On the mention of a stool wife, the kingmakers and some of the elders gave a prolonged laugh. This is because it reminded them of Nene Tsatsu's opposition to this kind of marriage. He gave a smile too, and then continued, 'this tradition also if it was beneficial during the time of our ancestors, then it was because they lived in a closed society; a society in which the only people they knew were those around them. Now, we live in an open and civilized society in which we always meet many different types of people we can associate with. Secondly, marriage, as instituted by God Himself, is for life and in order to sustain it, love must prevail between the man and the woman. Therefore the most important thing in marriage is love. It is not the families the couple come from or the amount of money each has. In fact, money is secondary in marriage. Therefore if money and prestige is used to entice a person into marriage, then it is no more marriage based on love. It becomes selling and buying of a property, and you all know that we cannot sell God's creation.'

'Therefore, it is not proper for parents to choose partners for their daughters or sons, or to force them to accept people of their choice. The best thing is to allow their daughters to find the one they feel they are genuinely in love with. After all, they are going into the marriage and not the parents. Parents can play a role in the choice but it should be on advisory basis only.'

'My elders, just like an arranged marriage, the practice of a stool wife also needs considering. If the chief is already married, I do not think it is wise to ask him to marry again, in the name of a stool wife. A wife is a wife, and so the already married woman should be taken as a stool wife as well. If the man is not already married, then he can be asked to take such a wife. But he must be given time to find the woman he really loves.'

Nene Tsatsu then paused for a while and asked his elders to be patient with him because he had a few more practices to talk about. He was asked to carry on and so Nene Tsatsu continued:

'The next tradition that I am worried about is the stigma that is branded people who suffer accidental deaths. I do not know what prompted our ancestors to initiate this practice, but so far as I am concerned, it has no place in modern society. One thing we have to know is that life is a risk; unless we decide to stay within our four walls all the time. But once we step out of our homes, we are risking our lives, and anything can happen to us, including an accidental death. Again, the use of science and technology has exposed us to many risks. This means that we are more at the risk of an accidental death than ever before.'

'Therefore if one dies of an accidental death, we should not despise him and treat him with dishonor, as an outcast. People say such a death is an abomination, but it is not. An accidental death is an unpreventable occurrence and so if it does happen, we should give the victim the same normal honors and ceremonies accorded those who die naturally.'

One of the elders asked permission from Nene Tsatsu to speak. When he got up, he did not make a speech; rather he asked a question. He asked Nene Tsatsu whether he was talking about honoring people who die accidentally because of the deaths of the late Kwam and Akortorku. Some of the elders glanced at each other but nobody said anything. In his response, Nene Tsatsu told his elders that they could take the recent cases of Kwam and Akortorku as typical examples of what he was talking about. But one thing he wanted them to know was that the practice was not enhancing peace and social cohesion. Then he went on:

'Again, there is the need to educate our people against the belief in witchcraft. Whenever a person dies, the death is attributed to the work of witchcraft, and this is often traced to a person in the village, in most cases a woman. What follows this is, to me, is barbaric. The woman is chased up and down and beaten up; and this sometimes ends in death. I do not know how this belief started but you will agree with me that this practice has no place in a modern society.'

'Many people have died out of negligence and ignorance as a result of illiteracy, and not the work of a witch. Therefore we have to educate our people to keep their environments tidy, and to be very conscious of their personal hygiene to minimize the chances of getting sick and dying suddenly.'

'There is a hospital at Kesua and now we have a clinic here in Adoma where we can go for treatment when we are sick. But what I have seen is that our people do not like going to hospital. Even when they are seriously sick, they stay at home and depend on herbs. And since herbs do not cure all sicknesses, these sick people needlessly die. What happens next is that the poor woman over there is taken as a witch and accused of being the cause of the death. Then she is attacked and beaten up. This is not only a social offence but also a criminal one. It is cruel and so it has no place in any civilized society.'

'You see, my elders, there were no clinics or hospitals during the time of our ancestors. So they had to treat their sick at home with herbs only, some of which were not the right ones. But now, we have hospitals or clinics in most places. Therefore nothing should prevent us from going to these health centers when we are sick.'

'We are not immune to sickness and so in our humanity, we are likely to be sick during the time of our lives. But unlike the time of our ancestors, we have places to go for treatment when we unfortunately get sick. Therefore, let us make use of these hospitals to prevent unnecessary deaths which might be caused by us, and not by that poor woman considered to be a witch. The problem is illiteracy and so we need to educate our people to understand the true situation and change their thinking. I will end here and allow anyone who has any contribution to make to do so.'

Goku, one of the clan leaders got up and said with all apologies that he was against most of the things Nene Tsatsu talked about. According to him, Nene Tsatsu was just trying to do what all western educated people do; which was to condemn their traditional ways of life. That was exactly what the white people did when they first came to their land, he reminded them. And so he did not think that should be allowed to continue.

Any condemnation of their traditional values would mean a condemnation of the ancestors, he reminded his colleagues. That would be a big mistake on their part because it was their ancestors' values that had guided and sustained them over the years. And so the ancestors could not have been wrong; otherwise they would not have been alive. Therefore, if they continued to question the practices handed over to them, he feared their ancestors would be crossed with them and the retribution would be unbearable.

Goku reminded his colleagues of what happened at Sonson some time ago when the people disobeyed their ancestors. For a whole year, a plague swept through the whole village, killing only the men. It was when the people realized their offence and the gods were appeased that the plague ceased. Therefore, Goku did not want the council to do anything that would bring a similar curse to Adoma.

Linguist Nanor was the next to speak. *He thanked Nene Tsatsu for calling their attention to the traditional practices that* he thought needed *considering.* He also thanked Goku for what he said in response to Nene Tsatsu's speech. But he said he missed the point in saying that Nene Tsatsu just wanted to condemn their customs. Nanor pointed out that the purpose of the meeting, which Nene Tsatsu made clear to everybody at the beginning of the meeting, was to examine the practices and find out which ones were relevant or irrelevant to their society.

Therefore, to him, the chief did not condemn any of the practices he talked about. He only expressed his opinions about them. So he called upon the elders to do the same thing so that they could come out with a joint decision as to whether to modernize those that were not enhancing societal cohesion, or abolish them. Then he told the elders that he was in support of the concerns raised by Nene Tsatsu about the traditions he mentioned in his speech. He cautioned that if they wanted a peaceful and progressive society, then the traditional practices found to be impediments in their progress should be modernized or replaced.

Then to support his argument, Nanor cited an example of an incident which brought a terrible strife in the village some years back. The problem was started by two families during the reign of the late chief. One of them lost a member who was sick for about six months, it was said. Soon after the child's death it was rumored that a woman, who was considered a witch, was the cause of the child's death. This rumor went on to spread until a member of the bereaved family said it in public, and was heard by a relative of the accused woman. Obviously, nobody would like to be accused of being a witch and so the woman and her husband felt their reputation was at stake. So in their wild anger they rushed to the house of the bereaved family to register their protest against the accusation.

A row then erupted which escalated into a serious warfare between the couple and the bereaved family people.

It spread very quickly, and soon there were reinforcements from both sides. And so this incident which started with a rumor degenerated into a family war. The late chief had to call in the local authority police before peace could be restored. When the case was later taken to the traditional court, the bereaved family could not prove the allegation against the accused woman. So it was found guilty and fined heavily.

Nanor revealed that since that time he had been thinking of how to make people realize the adverse effects of some of their traditional beliefs on society, like the belief in witchcraft. He was therefore happy that Nene Tsatsu had raised the issue. So he appealed to the elders to give their support to the idea of re-examining their practices in the interest of their society. Then in an advice, Nanor asked members to be frank in expressing their opinions so that they could take a realistic appropriate decision. After Nanor had spoken, Nene Tsatsu said everyone was free to express his views because that was the reason why he called for the meeting. But the debate which started as expression of opinions soon developed into a heated argument.

Members became divided into two groups; one supporting the traditions as instituted by their ancestors, and the other which wanted changes to be made in the interest of development.

The traditionalists wanted their traditional beliefs to be maintained. They said their ancestors tried them, saw that they were beneficial to society and had passed them on to them. So they owned them a duty to continue with the relay and not to break it. Breaking away from what their ancestors had toiled to institute for them, they argued, would be an abomination and a curse on them, something they did not want to happen to them.

The reformers were grateful to the ancestors for instituting the traditional practices but said that there was the urgent need for changes to be made. That was because some of the practices were causing discord in the village which was not enhancing social cohesion and economic development. They gave many examples of the practices that they believed were not bringing peace and cited many instances of unfortunate and tragic incidents, which they argued, occurred because of their adherence to those beliefs.

Among the many practices cited to support their argument was the prejudice against albinos. They argued that the belief that albinos were cursed by the gods to be witches and as a result they were not accepted by society was wrong. Because of that belief, albinos and their families always lived in fear; fear of being looked down upon, kidnapped, or worst still, assaulted. This, the reformers stressed, was against human rights to life and the will of God. It was not enhancing love for one another and peace in the village. So they wanted that belief, and many others, to be re-examined and eradicated if necessary.

The argument between the two groups degenerated into personal attacks as if some of the people had personal scores to settle with each other. Nene Tsatsu did not like the disgusting direction the debate was taking and so he had to exercise his authority to halt proceedings. When sanity was restored, he did not shrink away from telling the elders how disappointed he was to know some of them were still relishing in everything that their ancestors did so many years ago.

Nanor quickly responded to Nene Tsatsu's disappointment. On behalf of all members, he apologized to their chief for the way some of them were drifting into attacks on each other. He agreed with him that the behavior they displayed was out of order but he appealed to him to overlook it so that they could go ahead with the debate.

Nene Tsatsu then reiterated that the meeting was not for the condemnation of their traditions but to review them. The re-examination would enable them to identify those that were still necessary and helpful in a modern society and those that were irrelevant for a final decision to be taken. Then he referred the elders to what they told him at the beginning of the meeting; that they had to change the procedure of choosing their chiefs in order to crown him. That was because, he reminded them, as an educated person they believed he could lead them to bring prosperity to the village. If what they told him was really the reason for the change, then if they wanted social and economic progress, it was equally necessary for them to review their traditional practices.

He stressed that for a society to progress, peace and harmony had to prevail in families, between families, and in the entire village. But from what he had seen and heard over the years, Adoma had never been systematically peaceful. Their peace was always punctuated by quarrels in families between sons or daughters, and parents; or between one family and the other which, in most cases, resulted in conflicts. That warfare in a society, Nene Tsatsu went on would not enhance progress. And so since most of the problems were caused by people's strict adherence to their traditional practices, it was necessary for them to make reforms.

'What is the use of keeping something if it gives you problems all the time?' Nene Tsatsu asked his elders.

He then laid down guidelines for the continuation of the discussion. Anyone who had any concerns with any of the traditional practices or beliefs should bring them up for a debate, he directed. Everyone would be heard, and a vote would be cast either for its maintenance, reformation, or abolition, by a show of hands. This procedure was followed and at the end, a majority of the elders agreed that six of the traditional beliefs and practices identified, should either be reformed or ditched.

These included: The practice of not sending first born-males or females to school; the practice of parents choosing husbands for their daughters; and the tradition of mandatory stool wife. Others were the belief that witches were the cause of deaths in the village; the belief that an accidental death occurred as a result of a curse by the gods; and the prejudice against albinos because of the belief that they were witches. The six practices identified were to be taken to the general meeting with the people where a final decision would be taken on them.

Nene Tsatsu congratulated the elders on the agreement they had reached, and saluted them for the unprecedented wise decision they had taken. First they decided to make him their chief because they believed he could bring transformation to the village. Then in order to accelerate the development they so much wanted, they again took another decision to try as much as possible to eradicate from the society all the known traditional beliefs and practices that were hindering their progress. That was an indication of how determined they were to have their village developed, he told the elders. Then he added that by the steps they had taken, they had become agents of change and transformation which, he believed, other towns and villages might emulate.

As soon as a date had been scheduled for the meeting with the people, Goku raised an issue. He said he was apprehensive of a vengeance from the ancestors for the intended changes of the practices identified. Other elders expressed the same concern and fear, and suggested that the ancestors should be informed about the changes. They felt the information would let the ancestors know that they had not ignored them. But it was generally agreed that the information should wait until a final decision was taken at the meeting with the people.

Nene Tsatsu then made it clear to the elders that the decision they had taken was not the end of what they had to do. He told them the most important thing to do was the selling of the decisions they had taken to the people. He pointed out that the people had to be educated and convinced that the changes were inevitable if Adoma was to be developed into a progressive modern society; and be made to embrace the reforms. He knew it was not going to be an easy task but he believed that with proper education they would be able to achieve their aim. He therefore asked the elders to start educating the people without delay beginning with their family members. Education of the family members first was very vital because they could eventually join them to educate the general public, Nene Tsatsu pointed out.

Chapter 16

Nene Tsatsu pondered over the meeting he had with the clan leaders and the decision they arrived at, and he was pleased with the outcome of events. When he was installed as chief of Adoma, he vowed to try his best to justify the belief and confidence that the people had in him. He was told he was made chief because they knew he would be able to help develop and bring progress to the village. And so in order to justify the people's trust in him he had to deliver and yield good results. So he was optimistic that the decision they had taken would help build a society of peace and common understanding which would provide the necessary healthy atmosphere for him to continue to execute his developmental plans.

The next day during a normal family meeting, Nene Tsatsu briefed his wives on the decision he had taken with the clan leaders with regard to the unhealthy traditional practices. He made them understand that those practices were sowing discord in the society and retarding progress. Abla agreed with him, adding that she was very happy with the preliminary decision he and his elders had taken. She cited examples of horrible incidents that occurred in the village before Nene Tsatsu became chief which almost tore the village apart. The first was a case about marriage. In accordance to the belief that parents could best choose a man for a daughter to marry, a parent began to groom his daughter for a man from a rich family. After giving him assurances that he would have his daughter as a wife, this parent started accepting presents, including money, from him. And when he realized that his father-in-law to be liked money, he always lavished cash on him even if he did not ask for it. All these things were taking place without the knowledge of the daughter.

Meanwhile she continued to date the man she loved, unaware that her love was under threat. One day her parents sat her down and told her that she was old enough to get married. And then, to her amazement, she was informed that a husband had been found for her. She agreed with her parents that she was ripe to get married but said she would marry only the man of her own choice.

The girl's response infuriated her parents but they did not argue with her. Instead, they asked her to go and think of it; adding that they were in a better position to get a husband who would treat and look after her properly. In defiance, she ignored what her parents told her and continued to visit her boyfriend. One day she invited him to the house and introduced him to her parents as the one she would marry. That was the beginning of the crisis. The father became angry and said that what she had done was an insult to the family. Then turning to the man, he told him he was not worthy of marrying his daughter, and asked him not to visit her again.

When the father suspected that the girl was still meeting her man, he travelled all the way to his house and, in the presence of his parents, gave him a stern warning. The man's parents felt insulted and when they protested against his behavior, the father rather got incensed and a row ensued. The confrontation became so acrid that neighbors had to come in to intervene and the parent was asked to leave the house immediately.

Back home, he invited the man he had chosen for her daughter to his house and a date was fixed for the traditional marriage rites to be performed, against the wishes of the daughter. But a day before the scheduled date, the parents noticed her absence. She had eloped with the man she loved, and nobody had the slightest idea where they had gone to.

But that was not the end of the fracas between the two families. Each one accused the other of being the cause of the couple's disappearance. This accusation and counter-accusation engineered by relatives of both families developed into sporadic clashes which lasted for a long time. It became a subject of public concern and condemnation until the late chief issued a warning to both sides to stop disturbing public peace.

Later, it was a rumored that the couple escaped to the city and got married. Abla ended the story by telling Nene Tsatsu that the terrible suffering the couple went through would never have arisen if the parents had not tried to force their own choice of a man on their daughter. That was why she strongly supported a review of such a traditional practice.

Abla also told the chief about another deplorable incident that happened. A couple had an albino male child who was raised up without exposing him too much to the general public because they were afraid of the maltreatments that would be meted out to him by the public. It was a general belief that albinos were cursed by the gods to be in the condition they were in and so they were not accepted in public. So the boy was allowed to go out only in the company of adults to avoid the fierce hatred and attack against all albinos.

One day after school, when the boy was going home alone because a relative was unable to get to him on time, he was kidnapped. There were many frantic efforts by many concerned and worried people to find him or his kidnappers but all were in vain. The boy had never been found.

Abla could not understand why people should be allowed to live with that prejudice against albinos. She was, therefore, extremely happy that a decision had been taken to spurn it; together with other practices that were not promoting good morality and social cohesion. Naki also expressed her delight about the decision taken by the elders. But she admitted that it was not going to be easy to change the people's behavior and attitude.

Nene Tsatsu was amazed to hear the incidents Abla narrated. He responded by telling his wives that what he had heard from them had given him more encouragement to see that all repugnant beliefs were eradicated from the society. He knew it was going to be difficult but with dedication and strong commitment, he was positive it could be done. Then he informed his wives about the scheduled meeting with the people and charged them with the responsibility of spearheading the education of the women. He advised that after the general meeting, they could hold other meetings with the women and educate them on the evil and anti-social practices that needed to be reformed.

Six days before the meeting, Nene Tsatsu met with his traditional councilors to settle a case brought by a wife against her husband. The wife, Dede, noticed a strange change of behavior in Kofi which was a surprise to her. He always went out in the evening and came back home very late. Sometimes, he would not eat her food, and his concern for her started to wane. She did not know why that strained relationship should start all of a sudden and threaten their marriage.

Whenever she asked Kofi what the problem was, he always said nothing was wrong. But she suspected that Kofi was flirting with another woman and when she confronted him about it one day, Kofi flared up. In his anger, he asked her what she wanted him to do since she could not bear him children. Dede wept bitterly the whole day. She felt she had been insulted and disgraced by Kofi and so she took the case to Nene Tsatsu so that he could clarify his statement before the chief.

When Dede narrated her side of the problem between the two, Kofi was also asked to tell the council about the cause of their strained relationship. He did not deny what she had said. But he explained that he took the action out of pressure from friends and family members. That was because he had married her for five years but she was not able to give him children and he could not bear the ridicule and the shame of not having a child. So he went to an oracle to find out from the fetish priests what the cause of their inability to have children was. And to his utter disappointment he was told that a witch had turned his wife's womb upside down and so she would never be able to get pregnant. Therefore, since he wanted to have children to show that he was a man, he made up his mind to take another woman. But he decided to keep it secret until he was ready to marry her.

The councilors asked the couple many questions, most of which were directed to Kofi. Then Nene Tsatsu summarized everything to make the situation clear to them. He sympathized with both of them and said the situation they were in was not caused by either of them. He told them it was a societal problem; the belief in the society that any negative thing that occurred in the village was caused by a witch. That idea had to be discarded because it was a misconception, Nene Tsatsu stated.

Then he stated that misfortunes could happen through natural or human causes. Human causes could be either as a result of mistakes or ignorance, and that the couple's problem was that of ignorance. So in order to know exactly what the cause of their inability to have children was, he suggested that both of them should see a doctor for medical examination. He made them understand that the doctor would be able to find out after the tests if any of them actually had a child-bearing problem.

Dede was pleased with the explanation and the suggestion given but Kofi seemed unconvinced. Nene Tsatsu noticed that he was not impressed and so he offered to contact the hospital for an appointment date on their behalf. He also promised to ask one of his councilors to go to the hospital with them. Meanwhile, he would like them to be patient and continue to stay together peacefully as they used to do. With this advice, the couple left the palace.

Nene Tsatsu was then briefed by his councilors on the self-help projects being undertaken. He was pleased to hear that the spirit of the people was high, and that work was going on harmoniously. That was exactly what he wanted. He was also glad that some of the councilors had already started preparing the people's mind for the intended meeting with them. All the reports Nene Tsatsu received indicated that many people would be happy to see the negative traditional beliefs erased from the society. That did not mean that they were not going to have a hostile opposition but he felt it was a hope they could hold on to.

Other matters discussed at the meeting included the progress of the on-going projects and the fundraising activities toward the purchase of the corn-mill, as decided. Nene Tsatsu was over the moon to hear that the donations they had already received could buy two corn-mills instead of one. He considered that information an indication of the people's enthusiasm and determination to undertake progressive projects that would improve their living standards.

Nene Tsatsu revisited the case they deliberated on earlier, concerning the couple. He made it known to the councilors that he was extremely delighted the problem was brought to them before the date scheduled for the meeting with the people. It was an excellent case to be used to support their fight against the unproductive traditional practices.

Then he revealed that that was the reason why he offered to help Kofi and Dede with the hospital appointment. He therefore asked Linguist Nanor to see him in the morning for a letter which he should take to the hospital for the appointment. They had a week more for the meeting with the people and he wanted to medical examination to be conducted before the meeting day.

After that, Nene Tsatsu produced a letter from the Chief Executive of the District Council, Kesua, and gave it to Nanor to read to all members. He opened the letter and started reading it:

'Dear Nene Tsatsu 111,

'The central government has been following the social and economic activities in Adoma with the greatest interest and has noted with pleasure the developments that are emerging in the village of Adoma under your dynamic leadership.'

'The self-help projects that you and your people are embarking on in order to improve the living standards of your people are exactly what government would like all communities to do.'

'Just as the biblical adage goes, God helps those who help themselves, government is prepared to assist all communities that are making an effort to develop their neighborhoods.

'Therefore in recognition and appreciation of your exemplary achievements, government has directed the district Council to extend electricity and water supplies to all parts of Adoma with immediate effect.

'Government will continue to follow with keen interest, all projects that you and your people will or are undertaking. If they are considered to be in favor of social and economic advancement, government will not shrink away from coming to your assistance, technically or financially.

'It is hoped that you will continue to mobilize your people for more projects that will eventually transform Adoma into a modern town. What an achievement that would be!

'Your information concerning potential deposits of minerals in the lowlands of Adoma was received with keen interest. Very soon government will be sending prospectors to the area to determine its mineral potentialities. It is hoped that they will be given the fullest cooperation.'

'I wish you and all the people of Adoma, all the best.'

'Yours faithfully,
Tetteh-Wayo
(Chief Executive)
District Council, Kesua.'

There was a spontaneous applause to show how delighted members were when Nanor finished reading the letter. One could see them talking to each other and nodding their heads in exultation. Even Nene Tsatsu could not help hiding a grin. When the contents of the letter were opened for a general discussion, almost all the councilors praised the government for recognizing what they were doing at Adoma and coming to their aid. But Nene Tsatsu said the greatest praise should go to them, the councilors, and all the people of Adoma for their cooperation and determination to have Adoma developed. He stressed that for a community or country to progress, the prerequisite necessity was cooperation. So he thanked his councilors and all the people of Adoma for the support they were giving him.

The councilors were equally happy that their village had attracted the attention of the central government when they got to know that prospectors would be coming to Adoma. All of them hoped that the outcome of the exploratory work would be positive and government would start mining work in the village soon. That would be a boost to Adoma's social and economic development, it was noted. To prepare for the visit, Nene Tsatsu asked Linguist Nanor to arrange for a meeting with all landowners whose lands stretched into the areas to be prospected.

Chapter 17

The following day, Nanor came for Nene Tsatsu's letter and went to the district hospital at Kesua together with Kofi and Dede, as already agreed. Luckily, the hospital was not so busy and so after waiting for a few hours, they were asked to go to see the doctor. Nanor went into the consulting room with the couple and handed over the letter to him. But the doctor explained to him that it was purely a personal matter and the outcome of the examination would be confidential. So he advised him to go back to the reception and wait for the couple.

The doctor had a few minutes interview with Kofi and Dede in order to know each person's medical history, and that of their families. Then he called a nurse and asked Dede to go with her for tests to be done on her. While that was going on, he asked Kofi to go to the back of the curtain where he did some tests on him. When the nurse completed her tests on her, she brought her back to the consulting room. By that time the doctor too had finished part of the tests on Kofi, and so he asked the nurse to go with him to do the rest of the tests. That gave him time to complete Dede's examination.

When all the medical tests were completed on both of them, the doctor asked the couple to relax while he studied the test results. This took about half an hour. When he became sure of his findings, he revealed the results to them, beginning with Dede's. He informed her that there was nothing wrong with her. She was fertile and so she would be able to bear children. The couple received the information with mixed reactions. It filled Dede with massive joy and relief. She turned and looked at Kofi, and then exclaimed: 'I am vindicated; there is no witch preventing me from having children; thanks be to God.' Kofi on the other hand expressed an emotion of shock. That was not what he expected to hear. His fetish priest had told him Dede was barren; her womb had been turned upside down and so she could not bear children. That was what he wanted to hear.

So he asked the doctor whether what he had told them was the absolute truth. He thought Kofi asked the question out of excitement, and so he told him that all the tests on Dede proved positive and that she could have as many children as she wanted. The only thing was that, as a couple, they had a problem which would delay their child bearing, the doctor continued. And that problem was not with her but with Kofi. Then he revealed to them that Kofi's tests showed that he had a low sperm count and that was the reason why they were unable to have children. But he asked them not to worry too much because the problem was not at its advanced stage and so it could be remedied. Kofi could not believe what the doctor said as seen from his facial expression. Realizing this, the doctor assured him that his problem could be cured and so he was going to make an arrangement for him to start treatment immediately.

When the appointment date was scheduled, he put a copy of the test results into an envelope, sealed it and gave it to Kofi. Then he advised him not to fail to come back for treatments and further tests whenever he was asked to do so. He assured him again that he could regain his manhood power and libido after the treatments. Then while the couple was still in the consulting room, he wrote a cover letter and when he was seeing them off, he gave it to Nanor to be given to Nene Tsatsu. When the trio returned to Adoma, Kofi and Dede did not go straight to their house. They were aware that the doctor gave a letter to Nanor to be given to the chief. So they decided to go with him to the palace to find out if he had something to tell them.

Nene Tsatsu was extremely pleased with the results of the medical examination because of two reasons. He was happy that Kofi's problem of child birth could be remedied, according to the doctor. Secondly, he was pleased to hear that there was nothing wrong with Dede with regard to child birth. To him, it was a great triumph for her and for the society as a whole because it dispelled the belief that misfortunes, like inability to have children, were caused by witches.

Seeing that Kofi did not look so happy, he advised him to cheer up and take the doctor's findings in good faith. He told him that he knew of a few people who had similar tests and were found to have the same problem. But the good news was that, like the doctor said, their problems were solved and they were able to have children. Therefore, he believed that Kofi, too, would be able to bear children after the treatments. Then in his final admonition to the couple, he advised them to keep the doctor's findings only to themselves, and take the medical treatments seriously.

Before their departure, Nene Tsatsu asked permission from the couple to use their visit to the hospital to support his case during the meeting with the people. He said he wanted to use it to back the argument that misfortunes, like theirs, were not the work of witches. He assured them that he would not mention their names, and that he would only talk about what the juju man told Kofi, their going to the hospital and what the doctor found out. His aim was that their story would help dissuade the general public from believing that witchcraft could make a woman infertile. They were happy with the request and so Nene Tsatsu's permission was granted.

When the meeting day came, many people turned up at Laasi Park to hear what Nene Tsatsu had to say. He began his speech by thanking the people for their unflinching cooperation and for coming to the meeting. Then he announced that in recognition and appreciation of what they were doing to develop Adoma, government had directed the Council to extend electric and water supplies to all parts of Adoma. The long thunderous applause and shouts of appellation that followed his announcement echoed far and wide. Somebody in the crowd shouted: 'That is great. Our wells will then be white elephants soon.'

When the applause and the jubilation ended, Nene Tsatsu reminded the people of the suspected mineral deposits in the area. Then he informed them that government would soon be sending prospectors to the village to ascertain whether it would be worthwhile to start a mining industry in Adoma. This information, too, was warmly received by the people. They knew any government industry in the village would advance its progress and open it to all parts of the country, and indeed the entire world.

Nene Tsatsu saw that the pieces of information he gave to the people had put them in a very happy mood. So he felt time was ripe for him to introduce the main topic for the meeting. He began by telling the people that before he would talk about the main reason why he had called them for the meeting, he would like to tell them two stories. Then he went on:

'A long time ago,' he began to tell the first story, 'there was a couple who had been married for years but they were unable to have children. So there was nothing to bind them together except for the profound mutual love that initially brought them together. After some time, that deep love started to wane as a result of unbearable pressure on the man from his parents. They wanted their son to bear children so that they could have the pleasure of playing with their grandchildren before they joined their ancestors. Since the parents continued to pile pressure on him to look for another woman, if the one he had could not bear children, their love continued to fall apart.

'One day the man went to a fetish priest to find out why they were unable to have children and the juju man told him that his wife had a problem. A witch had turned her womb upside down and so she could never be pregnant. A man exclaimed: 'How can we prevent these witches from destroying us?' Another man responded: 'The fetish priests are not always right.'

Nene Tsatsu continued: 'The man believed what he was told and so he secretly went into a relationship with another woman and started ignoring his real wife. She tried to find out why her husband had changed his attitudes toward her but he would not open up to her. And so in her frustration and desperation, she went to confide in their local church priest. The priest called the couple for a meeting and after some hours of talks, he was able to convince them to go to a hospital for a medical check-up. He made them understand that it was only after a medical examination that a doctor could find out why a couple could not bear children.

The couple took the priest's advice and so an arrangement was made for them for the medical examination. They went as scheduled and the tests were done. But contrary to what the fetish priest told him, the man was informed that it was he who had a problem, and not the wife. His sperm count was low and that was the cause of his inability to impregnate his wife. However, the doctor assured him that his problem was not incurable. He made another arrangement for him to start immediate medical treatments and he went through the medical treatments religiously as directed by the doctor. And within a short time, he regained his manhood strength. All this time his wife stood by him without going astray.

Nene Tsatsu ended his story by telling the people that when he last heard of the couple, they had borne three beautiful and vibrant children. Then he said his second story was not a story as such. It was something that happened in the village not long ago, which he wanted to remind them of. He stated that it was not proper to remind people of painful memories but he would like to bring their minds back to the accident in which the late Asawatse Kwam died.' Then he went on:

'Most of us were at the scene on that fateful day and we saw that what happened was indeed an accident. But the late leader was not given the normal funeral rites to honor him. This is because of the belief that unnatural deaths are the result of curses inflicted on people by the gods, for their evil deeds. So when there is death like this, the dead as well as his family members, and the entire community suffer from shame and distress. This is because the dead is treated ignominiously. I do not think we should allow a belief like this to make people suffer and deprive them of honor.'

'No. Nene, that belief is wrong. It is giving us problems,' said a man from the audience. This was followed by other inaudible responses from the crowd.

Murmurings could still be heard when Nene Tsatsu continued with his speech. He told the people that he chose to tell them about the two incidents because both of them had the same central theme of a traditional belief. Then he said it was good for people to have a belief but that belief must be one that brought peace and harmony in the society. But as they could see from the two incidents: the belief that people were unable to have children because of the work of a witch was not only baseless but also divisive. If the couple had not been advised to go for medical tests, the man would have stuck to that belief and, eventually, the marriage would have broken down.

In the case of the death of Kwam, Nene Tsatsu said there was no need to go to see a juju man or a doctor for a medical test for a proof. That was because most of them were at the scene and saw that what happened was an accident; an accident caused by a human being and not the gods. Therefore the belief that tragic deaths occurred because the victims were cursed by the gods, to him, was baseless just like the belief that witches were responsible for people's inability to give birth to children. So he made them realize that instead of helping to live happily in peace and unity, some of their practices were rather sowing discord in the society.

Nene Tsatsu felt his introductory lesson had prepared the people's minds for the topic of the day. So he informed them that it was because of the traditional beliefs and practices, such as the two mentioned, that he had called for the meeting. Then he told them that for a society to be prosperous, the people's beliefs and practices had to promote the basic necessity of peace and harmony. But, regrettably, Nene Tsatsu went on, he had seen that many of their practices were doing more harm than good. Instead of promoting peaceful existence, some of them were rather bringing hardships and dividing the society. He warned that if they continued to cherish such beliefs and practices, consistent peaceful atmosphere would not prevail for social and economic development to take place.

He said he knew how eager they were to have the village developed, but to be frank, in order to speed up progress, the traditional beliefs and practices that were causing dissension and disharmony in the society had to be reviewed. And In order to do that, he informed them that he met with his councilors and a list of such unhealthy beliefs and practices had been compiled. So he would like Linguist Nanor to read out what he had on the list to them so that those who had anything for or against the listed practices, could air their views. After that, a general decision would be taken as to whether to maintain the beliefs and practices, reform or outlaw them.

Nene Tsatsu's announcement was received with mixed responses. While the moderates in the community happily hailed the reformation as a reasonable action that would help move the village forward, the traditionalists thought otherwise. They said the action the council members had taken was an abomination and asked whether members had the power to override what the ancestors had instituted. But they were told that what the elders had done was just a proposal. All the practices in question would be discussed at the meeting, and so they should wait to air their views during the debate.

Linguist Nanor then read out the practices that were of grave concern to the council members. These included the practice of arranged marriage which was bringing discord in families and the community; the practice of not sending first-born sons to school because parents wanted them to cultivate the land with them, and take over their assets when they were gone; and the tradition of taking a stool wife, even if a chief already had one. Others were the belief that any misfortune that occurred in the society was caused by a witch; the belief that tragic deaths were the result of curses by the gods, and so the victims were treated with dishonor; and lastly the prejudice and ill-treatment against albinos who were considered to be cursed by the gods.

Nanor reminded the people that the council members only identified the beliefs and practices that they felt were giving the whole community problems. What should be done about them would be decided by all the people present. So he invited those who had any concerns for or against the practices to speak out.

A majority of the people spoke favorably either for total abolition or reformation of the beliefs and practices. Those who spoke vehemently against the eradication of the practices said the changes would risk the wrath of the gods and the ancestors. They argued that the ancestors toiled hard to institute the practices which had guided them over the years, and so they felt their abolition would bring disastrous consequences. They cited an example of a case in one of the neighboring villages in which the ancestors unleashed vengeance on the people for their disobedience and negligence. For years, there was famine in which many people died. It was after the people had got to know the cause of their predicament and the gods were appeased that the famine ended. Therefore, they did not want that kind of a curse to be inflicted on the people of Adoma.

To allay the fears of those who were against the intended changes, Nanor informed them that the council members had already considered all the concerns they raised. They were aware of the tremendous contributions the ancestors had made toward their very existence. So they would not do anything that would trigger their anger. Therefore, after a final decision had been taken the ancestors would be informed of their action.

Nene Tsatsu then reiterated that if the people really wanted harmony and progress in Adoma, changes in the traditional beliefs and practices that hinder peace and stability could not be compromised. He admitted that the changes would be an uphill task but he said he was optimistic that it could be done. When the debate continued, everybody was allowed to air his or her views on the proposed changes. Many more people spoke for or against the practices and at the end, it was agreed that a vote should be cast. That was done and the result was that a majority of the people agreed that the six traditional beliefs and practices discussed should be reformed.

These were the belief that albinos were witches, cursed by the gods and the general prejudice against them; the practice in which parents chose men for their daughters and force them to marry these men; the practice of mandatory stool wife, a wife that went with the installation of a chief; the belief that sicknesses and deaths were caused by witches; the belief that an accidental death was the result of a curse by the gods and so the dead was not given any honor; and the tradition of not sending first-born males to school because parents wanted them to understudy them so that they could inherit them when they were no more alive.

Measures were put in place by the people as to what to do to achieve their aim with regard to the decision taken. All of them were of the opinion that it would take a long time for the changes to be realized because the beliefs and practices had been with them for ages. But they were of the belief that with continuous education and counseling of the people, gradually, results would be achieved.

With regard to the belief that albinos were witches, the decision was that that belief should be abolished totally. The people were to be made aware of its evil effects; for an example, the distress it brought to the people concerned and their families. Besides, it was against human rights to live. Sometimes albinos were kidnapped and maltreated. That was a criminal thing to do. So because of this and other negative effects the people wanted this belief to be erased from the society completely. And this, it was agreed, would be done through education.

The people felt that parent's involvement in the choice of a daughter's husband was contrary to the intentions of the ancestors. The choices they were making were not in the best interest of their daughters, but in their own interest. And this was the money and the material things that they were getting personally, and the prestige that the family, as a whole, was enjoying. Therefore, parents would be advised to play only advisory and guidance role in their daughter's marriage. The final choice of the man should be the sole responsibility of their daughters.

With regard to the tradition of a stool wife, the reform was that if the new chief was already married, he should not be made to marry again if he did not want to. Even if he wanted to take another wife, he should be given time to look for the woman he felt he was really in love with.

The people were to be made to understand and discard the belief that sicknesses and deaths were caused by witches, through education. This would involve counseling people on the importance of personal hygiene to prevent sicknesses, and the necessity of getting medical treatment early when they were sick. It was realized that many people did not like going to hospital. Some of them always waited until the sickness was hopelessly serious before going to hospital to be treated. Then when the unfortunate thing happened, they would put the blame on an innocent woman whom they considered a witch. It was believed education would help clear that notion from people's mind and create an atmosphere of peaceful co-existence in the village.

Again through education, it was hoped that the people would get to understand that accidents could happen to anybody, anytime, anywhere through natural causes or personal error. That, it was believed, would make them realize that the gods did not play any role in accidents at all and, eventually, make them discard the belief that people suffered accidental deaths because they were cursed by the gods. Then that would pave the way for the normal funeral rites to honor victims of accidental deaths.

Parents would also be educated on the importance of formal education, and advised to send all their children to school, regardless of the order in which they were born. They were to be made to understand that education of their children would make them more enlightened and better people. And if they still wanted them to come back to help on the land, they would be better farmers and custodians to take over their parents' lands and property if they wanted to. It was believed that these measures would help parents to put an end to the tradition of not sending first-born males and women to school.

After the measures to be used to effect the changes were identified, a bottle of schnapps was provided and, as it was agreed upon earlier, libation was poured to inform the ancestors of the changes they intended to make. In it, Nanor paid a glowing tribute to the ancestors for the guidance they had been giving them over the years. Then he informed them that the changes were necessary because the traditional practices concerned were causing discord in the society and impeding social progress. And since they wanted them to live in peace and harmony to be able to carry on with the work they had started, they had to make the changes, he concluded. Then he asked for their blessings.

Nene Tsatsu was very happy with the outcome of the meeting. In his address, he thanked the people and told them that the decision they had taken was a very important one. But he said what they had done was not the end of what they had to do. In order to achieve their utmost aim, they had to educate their family members and neighbors on the merits and demerits of the traditional beliefs and practices to enable them embrace the changes.

A month after the meeting with the people, the traditional council met to evaluate the impact the changes were having on the general public. Nene Tsatsu was delighted to hear that most of the people the councilors spoke to were in favor of the reforms. He informed the councilors that he had asked his wives to take part in the education of the women. Then he reminded them that what all of them had to do was to try as much as possible to change the people's thinking. He said they could do that by proving to them that a belief or practice was credible or incredible; advantageous or disadvantageous to them and the society. It was when the people were absolutely convinced that the beliefs were not helping the society that they would be prepared to change, Nene Tsatsu stated.

Since changing of people's mindsets could take a long time to be accomplished, they expected the education of the people to take that long. Therefore, Nene Tsatsu suggested the building of a community center where people could conveniently meet for play, relaxation or the holding of adult education classes. This was agreed upon by all the councilors, and Linguist Nanor was asked to make arrangements for work to start.

Nene Tsatsu offered to contact sponsors for assistance, and one of the councilors was happy to offer a piece of his land for the building. Everybody was pleased with his offer because of the central location of the land.

Linguist Nanor then informed members that two corn-mills had been bought instead of one because the total amount of money realized was more than they expected. A decision was then taken to install the corn-mills at different locations so that many people would not have to walk long distances to use them. Nanor was therefore charged with the responsibility of looking for the two locations that would be convenient to the people. Not too long after, the two corn-mills were installed.

Chapter 18

Nene Tsatsu travelled to the city the following week to solicit assistance for the building of the community center. When he made a stop at the Ketu District Council to have a discourse with the Chief Executive, he was told that a letter was about to be dispatched to him concerning the visit of the government prospectors. That was great news to him. He was extremely happy the group would be arriving at the village in two weeks' time. In that joyous mood, he briefed the Chief Executive on the actions the people of Adoma had taken on the traditional beliefs and practices that were retarding their social and economic progress. Then he informed him about the community center the people wanted to build so that they could have a common place for social and educational activities.

The Chief Executive was pleased to hear of the latest ambitious venture he was undertaking, and praised him for his great courage and determination. He agreed with him that a common comfortable meeting place was indeed necessary and so he promised to give technical and material assistance for the work to be done. Similar promises were made to him by friendly companies and individuals when he got to the city. But his greatest joy emanated from the news of the arrival of the prospectors at the village. He knew that official declaration of mineral deposits in the area would encourage the government to start mining work in Adoma which would accelerate social and economic development. So he returned to the village that day, a very happy man, and started getting ready to receive the visitors.

The following day, Nene Tsatsu met with his councilors and gave them a briefing on his visit to the city; and his stop over at the District Council. In it, he informed his councilors that all the people he went to have dialogue with endorsed the building of the community center and made pledges of assistance to him. With regard to the visit of the officials from the Ministry of Energy and Mineral Resources, he told them their work would take three days, but they would be based at Kesua where an accommodation would be provided for them by the District Council. Then he asked all the council members to make themselves available on those three days so that they could take the prospectors round.

Already they had discovered some quantities of mineral deposits at the lowlands, and so Nene Tsatsu wanted more prospecting to be concentrated in those areas. Then after that he would like prospecting to be done on the Koro hills suspected to be rich in clinker. Asked if the landowners concerned were informed of the visit and what the people would be doing, Nanor informed him that all the landowners had been briefed on what the visitors would be doing. But Nene Tsatsu told his councilors that more still had to be done. Just as they had decided to educate the people on the need to do away with the beliefs and practices that were causing hardships in the society; they had to educate the landowners on the importance of allowing their lands to be inspected and, possibly, taken over by the government. The royalty the government would pay them might be huge, and the social and economic benefits to the village would be immense, Nene Tsatsu stressed.

That day was the day scheduled for the installation of the corn-mills. So at the end of the meeting, Nene Tsatsu and all the councilors went to the installation sites. Before they got to the first site, a group of people and the technicians had already gathered and structures had already been put up. The work was done by the technicians only. Interestingly, some of the women came to the site with bowls of corns so that they could be the first to use the corn-mills. When the installation was completed, Linguist Nanor allowed all those who brought bowls of corns to the site that day to have them milled for them free of charge.

In a statement which Nene Tsatsu considered a joke, he said he would be delighted to take porridge, prepared from the first batch of corns milled, for breakfast the next day. The woman whose corns were the first to be milled thought he meant what he said, and so she told the chief that she would prepare a delicious porridge in the morning and have it sent to him. Nene Tsatsu thanked her profusely, but made her understand, politely, that what he said was a joke.

He then thanked the people for their generous donations which had helped to purchase the two corn-mills, and their cooperation in the work they were doing to improve the quality of life in the village. He made them understand that a token fee would be charged for the use of the corn-mills to raise revenue for other projects; just as market tolls were being collected. But he made them understand that he was not the one to take a decision on how much to pay. That would be done by a committee of people who would be responsible for managing the operation of the mills.

When Nene Tsatsu became chief of Adoma, everybody expected him to make himself a demigod and sacrosanct. That was how the previous chiefs portrayed themselves which distanced them from the people. But soon the people of Adoma realized that he was a chief of a difference; a real chief of the people. They admired him for his simple way of life, his passion to work with and for the people, and his strong desire to see Adoma developed. So they were not surprised to see him at the project sites anymore.

The installations of the corn-mills were followed by a series of other projects in the village. The first was the building of the community center which Nene Tsatsu wanted to be used, among other things, as a place where social and adult education classes could be held. As usual, he was present when work first started. He was happy to see representatives from all the clans eager to take part in the community work. That was the spirit he wanted to prevail in the village.

While the work on the community center was going on, work on the extension of electricity and water supplies to all corners of Adoma, as authorized by the central government, started. And, surprisingly, the District Council which was responsible for the water and electricity extension project also started tarring the road from Kesua to Adoma. That was not mentioned to Nene Tsatsu when he visited the district office. However, he welcomed all the development projects with the greatest delight. The people of Adoma were equally extremely happy. Never had they seen projects taking place at the same time in the village before; and never had Nene Tsatsu, himself, expected the projects to be taking place simultaneously.

The work on the community center progressed steadily. There was no need for a rush because no time limit was put on it. All the people doing the work had their own professions which they engaged in for a living. Some of them were farmers while others were local builders and carpenters. So they came to do the community work only on the traditional work-free days which were Wednesdays and Saturdays.

The people and organizations that promised assistance did not fail to honor their promises because of the strong connections Nene Tsatsu had with them. As a result, materials were always available to be used by the workers. While the builders were doing their work, the carpenters were making the doors, windows, benches and chairs that would be used in the center. Occasionally Nene Tsatsu was on site to monitor the progress of work done and to applause and urge the workers on.

While the people were still working on the projects, another group of people arrived in the village. They were from the Ministry of Energy and Mineral resources. The government had sent them there to determine the potentialities of deposits of mineral resources in the area and report back to the ministry. Nene Tsatsu had been notified, and so arrangements were in place to receive them. After a warm reception at the palace, Nene Tsatsu briefed the prospectors on the mineral deposits in the low lands, and the suspected availability of clinker in the koro hills. The leader informed Nene Tsatsu of what exactly members were there to do; adding that at the end of their work, they would send a report of their findings to the Ministry of Energy and Mineral Resources. The report would then be studied after which a decision would be taken as to whether to go ahead with official mining or not. After the briefings, the group left the palace to begin their work, accompanied by Linguist Nanor and two other traditional council members.

When they left, Nene Tsatsu told the other council members how happy he was about the development of events taking place. At the time the people of Adoma were in the process of building a community center, the District Council began tarring the road to the village and extending water and electricity supplies to all parts of the village. Then just like icing on the cake, prospectors arrived to begin exploratory work on the suspected mineral deposits.

While all the projects were taking place, Nene Tsatsu carried on with his chieftaincy duties. Whenever he was not very busy at the palace, he would visit the project sites to give the workers moral support. But his visits were no more as regular as they were when he first became chief. That was because he was getting older. From the businesses he was performing at the palace and his interactions with people, he could recognize that some of the people's perception of their traditional beliefs and practices was waning. He realized that the number of cases involving witchcraft, prejudice against albinos, and parents' rejection of their daughters' lovers was dwindling. This gave him more hope that the decision taken on the traditional practices would eventually bear fruits.

When the community center was completed and the necessary furniture and equipment put in place, it was realized that a caretaker was needed to manage it. The need also arose for people who could lead group discussions or conduct adult education classes. The traditional council met and a request was made for volunteers; and the response was very great. Out of the many people who wanted to offer their services, seven were recruited. One of them was taken to be the caretaker and coordinator of all activities. The remaining six were to be group leaders or teachers who would lead group discussions or conduct the adult education classes; one on each day of the week, apart from Sunday.

The main reason behind the building of the center was to have a common place where people could meet to be educated on the changes being made to their traditional beliefs and practices. But the volunteers were told that the group discussions and adult education classes were not to be limited to traditions alone. Literary and health education lessons were also to be treated to help improve literacy and reduce ignorance of the people. When all arrangements had been completed, the volunteers were given time to organize the topics they would like to be treating. Then the operation of the community center commenced.

At the beginning, attendance was low but soon many people became very interested in the activities taking place; and so the number of participants started increasing. Regular reports reaching the council members always indicated that patronage was going on well. Nene Tsatsu was very pleased to hear that the people were showing interest in the use of the center. He was of the opinion that the enthusiasm they were showing would soon justify the aim of putting up the community center.

But just as he thought measures had been put in place to help accelerate his reforms concerning the people's traditional beliefs and practices; another thing, which he considered a problem, emerged. That was the problem of government bureaucracy and people's attitude to government work which, according to him, was delaying work. He was getting older and so he wanted the transformations in Adoma to be completed before he was too old to be moving about, or before leaving this earth. But the work concerning the tarring of the road and the extension of water and electricity supplies was not going on at the pace he wanted. He felt progress was moving at a snail pace. And any time he was able to check from the foremen why that was so, he was told one material or another had not yet arrived from the district office.

Nene Tsatsu also found out that the workers were not showing much zeal or seriousness toward the work they were doing. Also, he was surprised to infer from what he was told that, after all, it was government work they were doing. He who had worked for private companies before he became a chief, was of the belief that work was work; and so there should be no difference of attitude toward doing a government and private company work. Therefore, he considered the lack of seriousness of the workers at the two project sites unacceptable. He felt the workers behavior together with the bureaucracy at the district office was slowing down progress and this was making him frustrated.

But that was not the only thing making Nene Tsatsu unhappy. When the government prospectors completed their work, he was briefed before they returned to the city. In his briefing, he was made to understand that there was positive evidence to show that large deposits of minerals were available in the village which would necessitate commercial mining. He thought government would act on the report immediately and so based on what the prospectors told him and his own expectation, he started making arrangements to welcome the miners that might be coming to the village.

He called for his councilors and at a meeting, it was agreed that if mining was to take place in Adoma which they firmly believed because of the assurances given them by the prospectors; then the expected miners would need an accommodation. Nene Tsatsu then asked the councilors to advise the people to form cooperative groups and start putting up decent houses to rent to the expected influx of workers.

This was welcomed by many people and within a short time, new buildings started springing up. Those who could not put up completely new houses began renovating their old ones. Walls of the old ones were reinforced with cement coatings and then painted. Thatched roofs were replaced with corrugated iron sheets, and real locks were fixed to doors instead of padlocks. All these were done with the anticipation that the central government would endorse the mining exploratory report early and the expected mining work would start soon. In fact, Nene Tsatsu wanted this work, together with the tarring of the road and the extension of power supplies, to be completed in his time. He knew their completion would complement his achievements and help boost his curriculum vitae.

But for years after the prospectors had come and gone, there was no news from the central government. That was a baffle to him. He did not understand why it was taking too long to take a decision on the investigators report; or if it had been taken, why the decision was not communicated to him. So the thought of this and the long time it was taking the workers in tarring the road and extending water and electricity supplies to the village always baffled and frustrated him. Sometimes, it even made him irritated. But he was careful not to think too much about the delay to avoid getting a heart attack since he was no more a young man. He was an action man who believed in quick action and personal contacts to put through his plans and programs. These were the reasons why he was profoundly unhappy with the delays.

One day, his old friend in the city, Saki, came to visit him. When he told him about his concerns and worries and what he would like to do, Saki offered to take him to the city to find out what was happening to the mineral report. When they got to the Ministry of Energy and Mineral Resources, he was disappointed at what he was told. The report had to be studied by individual expects, and after that a committee would meet to analyze every aspect of it before a recommendation would be made. Then it would be taken to parliament to be debated before a budget would be provided if approved for the commencement of the project.

Nene Tsatsu was shocked to hear that for years after the prospectors had completed their work, the report had not even passed through its initial vetting stages. That added to his frustration. He attributed the long delay to government bureaucracy which he talked about earlier; a delay which he felt was uncommon in private institutions. So Nene Tsatsu returned to the village more dissatisfied and unhappy than ever.

Two years after his visit to the city, the tarring of the road and about half of the water and electricity extension work was completed. That gave him some satisfaction. The people of Adoma were equally extremely happy. Those who started using electricity and pipe-borne water for the first time were so delighted that they immediately disposed of the lanterns and kerosene they were previously using for light. Some of them even boasted that they were getting lights just like city dwellers. They thanked Nene Tsatsu for his hard work and good leadership which had resulted in Adoma looking like a model town.

But Nene Tsatsu was not in that joyous mood that much. He was still concerned about a full completion of the water and the electricity work, and central government's long delay in acting on the mineral report. But since he knew he could not influence a speedy action, he resigned himself to waiting.

While he was trying to cope with what he considered unnecessary delays, there arose another thing he had to deal with. That was discontent in the village. The people were unhappy because, in pursuance of the advice given them, they spent a lot of money in putting up new residential buildings or renovating old ones. They did this hoping that the mining work would start soon and there would be workers to rent the buildings to and recover their monies. But long after the houses were completed, they could not get tenants because the mining work had not taken off; and there was no way they could get back the money they had spent on the buildings. So they were very disappointed and angry with the members of the traditional council. They felt they were given a premature advice which made them spent money which they would not have spent at that time. Some of them even went to the extent of venting their anger on some of the members of the traditional council for ill-advising them.

When Nene Tsatsu heard of this, he immediately realized that lack of communication was the cause of the people's unhappiness and reaction. When he made a visit to the Ministry of Energy and Mineral Resources and got to know why there was going to be a delay in taking a decision on the mining project, he rightly came back to brief the councilors. But the possible delay was not communicated to the people.

So he quickly convened a meeting with a view to arresting the situation. At this meeting, he told the people he perfectly understood and shared their frustration; and apologized to them for keeping them in the dark. Then he explained the real situation to them and appealed to them to be patient. He reiterated that from what they already knew and what the prospectors told him, there were enough mineral deposits in the village to warrant a commencement of a mining project. Therefore he advised the people to bear with them and keep on waiting as he, too, was; and that one day the mining work would start and all of them would begin reaping its fruits. And so Adoma continued to wait and wait because there was no alternative.

Nene Tsatsu was made chief of Adoma with the expectation that as an educated person, he would be able to develop the village culturally, socially and economically. He therefore firmly hoped that the on-going education of the people to advance his social and cultural reforms would eventually transform the village into a more cohesive society. As far as progress in general was concerned, he believed that he was able to justify the trust that the people reposed in him, considering the number of the developments he had brought to the village. His wish, however, was that the mining work would start to boost the social and economic development which would crown his achievements.

So even in his old age, he still continued to wait and wait; like 'waiting for Godot,' which never arrived; hoping that one day a mining project in Adoma would become a reality in his life time. However, even if it started after he had gone to join his ancestors, he was optimistic that the people of Adoma would still give him post humors credit for it. And everyone would agree with him that with their gracious cooperation, he was able to transform the village beyond their expectation.